aloha lagoon

www.alohalagoonmysteries.com

D1715644

ALOHA LAGOON MYSTERIES

DEATH UNDER THE SEA

an Aloha Lagoon mystery

Rosalie Spielman

Mahalo, or many thanks, to:

My family and friends, near and far, for all the love and support. Special thanks go to:

My parents, for birthing me, and for being my first editors. (Literally and figuratively.)

My sister, my always available and helpful first reader. You told me you liked my "voice" before I even knew what that meant. I would never have gotten here without your encouragement, aka your stubborn refusal to let me give up. Thank you.

My brother, for giving me the inspiration for Kiki's "furnished lanai." Stay classy.

My kids, Spaghetti and the Yeti—you're the best and I'm proud of you! And yeah, I'm not cooking again tonight. Sorry, not sorry.

A very special thank you to my husband for his encouragement and support. I couldn't have done this without you, and honestly, wouldn't want to. I see a SkyTrak in your distant future.

My oldest and longest BFF, Phae—LYDBNQ! Thank you for your cheerleading.

My agent, Dawn Dowdle, I can't thank you enough for taking a chance on me and giving me these opportunities.

My publisher, Gemma Halliday Publishing, thank you for letting me join the world of Aloha Lagoon. I'm happy to be here!

My mentors, advice-givers, question-answerers, and confidence booster-ers: Amanda Flower, Barb Goffman, Korina Moss, Becky Corio, Grace Topping, Mrs. Lynch, Encyclopedia Brown, Miss Marple, and Google. Thank you for putting up with all my questions and helping me with that confidence thing.

My professional groups, the BRLA and the Chesapeake Chapter of Sisters in Crime. Thank you for celebrating with me.

My fellow writers of the WWACN, my first critique partners, thanks for laughing at my writing. I would never have kept going if you hadn't.

And to the passengers on the bumpy bus of writing, the gals of the HBWG. You've got two minutes to read this book, then it's back on the bus with you! Thank you for the fellowship.

Lastly, an extra special thank-you to the Aloha Lagoon Mysteries readers: Thank you for giving Kiki and me a chance. I hope you enjoy our story.

~ Rosalie Spielman

CHAPTER ONE

———

I stared at the void in front of me, the vast chasm deep, dark, and very, very empty. So much so, I thought, with a flutter of fear in my stomach, one could get lost forever.

Which would be *awesome*!

Except, this void was my purse. And though getting lost was my main goal in life at the moment, there was that small issue of food, drink, and lodging.

Sitting on the patio at the Aloha Lagoon Resort in beautiful Kauai, my cappuccino cooling, I watched the surf and pondered my next move. On the white sand, a blonde woman was teaching a girl how to maneuver herself on a surfboard, the gawky preteen's long limbs not cooperating very well.

I stretched, downed the last of my capp, and gave a quick wave to the waitress for another. I'd charge my breakfast to the room and figure it out later. I'd already decided I may as well go on the dive that was already paid for. It was why I was here, after all. But then…? Skip out on the resort and make a run from the bill? I shook my head. To where, and how would I get there? I could use my credit card, but the Barringtons would surely be alerted to my whereabouts, and that wouldn't do, now would it?

The waitress brought my drink and stopped at a table where a woman had recently sat. Her voice carried with the sea breeze, and my ears perked.

"Yes, I'll have a macchiato. Like the ones they make in Europe, a real one. Not those crimes of espresso those ridiculous chain coffee shops make."

I suppressed a smile. Her voice sounded a touch familiar, as well as her words. The woman sounded so like my mother, with her snooty way of talking and the accent dripping with "upper class." There was no way my mother would be here, though.

I snuck a peek at the woman. She looked midtwenties, like me.

Oh no.

I knew her. It was Ainsley Rickenbacker, of the Boston Rickenbackers. We used to hang out at Glory Gardens Prep. I slid down a bit in my chair and pulled the brim of my straw hat down before taking another glance.

Yup, that was her, in all her fake-blonde, fake-tanned, vapid glory. Her long blonde hair was so obviously fake. Not just tasteful highlights, like my hair...and my tan was real. She and her best friend used to gossip about everyone. There was zero chance I could stay incognito if she spotted me.

Down on the beach the surf lesson was over, and the pair were walking their boards up the beach. They waved their goodbyes, and the woman turned my way, her long sandy blonde hair flying out with her movement. A smile lit up her face, but when I turned to see who she was smiling at, I wanted to disappear.

It was the hot bartender from The Lava Pot, the one who very gently let me know last night that my card no longer worked. Would he rat me out if he saw me here, presumably eating on the same defunct card? I slid down more in the chair and pulled my hat down farther to hide my face better, wishing I had at least put my hair up to look a little different. He apparently didn't see me. He only had eyes for the surf instructor. At least until after they greeted each other *very* warmly, lucky girl, and then headed back toward me, hand in hand. There was no way he wasn't going to see me now.

"Oh, good morning." He stopped at my table and was gazing down at me. "Did you get everything worked out with your credit card?"

Doing my best to channel the supremely unflappable Mrs. Barrington of the Manhattan Barringtons, I nodded. "Oh, of course. All is well. Had them send me a new one."

"Must be nice." He had a very yummy English accent. "This is Samantha." He gestured to the woman. "And I'm Casey."

The girl focused her brown eyes on at me, frowning, but murmured a hello. I responded with a nod. Then she tipped her head. "Didn't I see you in the boutique this morning?" She had a rather annoying Australian accent.

"Just browsing," I gushed. "So many lovely things. I just couldn't make up my mind." In reality, I was asking about consigning some high-end labels, but apparently they weren't interested in used Louboutins. These two didn't need to know that small detail though.

I took a sip of my cappuccino in order to surreptitiously look at Ainsley. I straightened in surprise. She was gone, leaving her drink behind. No, two drinks. She'd been waiting for someone. As if to confirm, the waitress appeared carrying two plates, looked around, sighed, and carried them back inside.

I rubbed my forehead. Ainsley was probably here in Kauai with her gossipy BFF, Claire, and had run off to tell her she saw me. Next would be the texting, the instant messaging, the posting on social media… I was doomed.

"You okay?" asked Samantha. "You look like you've seen a ghost."

I waved her off, made a show of looking at my Cartier watch, then stood. "Well, it was nice to meet you, but I have an excursion at nine. I must be going now." I turned and did my best to grandly swoosh away but ran smack dab into a tall Hawaiian man. Quite a good-looking one, too.

"Well, hello there," he laughed, catching me by the upper arms and gently holding me away from him. His tanned skin was smooth and his dark hair almost to his shoulders. He wore a Hawaiian-print shirt open over a tank top, and there was a bit of a tattoo peeking out on his chest. That instantly made me wonder what the rest of it looked like—the tattoo and the chest.

Wowza.

"Well"—I lowered my voice into what I hoped was a husky seductive tone—"hello to you, too." And then I had a coughing fit. Trying to reclaim my dignity, I gave a little tip of my head before sashaying away, this time bumping into a table with my hip.

Stupid hip.

"Ow," I muttered as I hurried inside. Hopefully, the rest of my day would go better.

After stashing my valuables in the hotel safe, I put on

my swimsuit, wrapped a Hawaiian-print sarong around me, and arranged my long, light brown hair with its balayage highlights in a braid that fell down my back. I packed up a backpack with my diving equipment. I certainly didn't need a wet suit in this climate, unlike last month on the Australian coast.

I'd worry about my lack of funds later. My phone still worked, though I'd turned the data off weeks ago and only used it with free Wi-Fi. But the slew of disposable debit cards…they no longer did. I'd apparently used them all to their extent. I'd asked the family financial manager on the sly to discretely pop some of my savings over into a covert account I could access each month, but apparently the plan was found out. I had so many places I still wanted to go diving, beautiful seas I wanted to explore. I was not ready to go back.

Diving always gave me a calm and better insight. Perhaps a sea turtle might inspire a solution.

Since the dive shop was just down the beach from the resort, I walked down the sand to get to there. The Aloha Lagoon Dive Shop was a bit of a shack but not in any worse condition than any other dive shop I'd seen. In fact, except for the feral chickens scratching in the dirt under a tree, it looked just like the dive shop in Panama from a week ago. A van was waiting next to the shop, and a man was loading the tanks into a small trailer after an older man on the porch checked their readings.

The older man looked up as I approached. "Good morning!" He smiled, his teeth perfectly white. When he stood, I saw how tall he was and, despite being older, very fit. "And who do we have here?"

"Good morning." I held out a hand. "I'm Kiki Hepburn."

"Oh, yes, of course. Let's do a little paperwork inside." He shook my hand. "I'm Kahiau, by the way." He pronounced it *Kah-hee-ew*.

I followed him inside. The walls of the wooden building were covered with ocean topography maps, charts of Hawaiian reef fish, and labeled photos of local species. He walked around the counter and gestured me closer. "I need to verify your certification," he said, holding out his hand for my dive log, which held my certifications.

Sighing inwardly, I pulled out my logbook, which held

my certifications, and handed it over.

He flipped through it, his eyes growing wider with each page. "My, you've been diving all over, haven't you? The Great Barrier Reef, Panama…and Texas?" He laughed.

I smiled. "It was a confined water dive in a man-made cement lake. A bit surreal, actually. That's where I did my deep water certification."

"What was Panama like?"

I shrugged. "I saw a barracuda, and dolphins swam alongside the boat. And the dive shop had a monkey."

"Nice." He flipped back to my certifications. His forehead creased. "I thought your name was Kiki Hepburn? This says—"

"Yes, Kiki is my nickname, and Hepburn…is what I'm going by…here." I glanced around, conscious of being overheard.

The man studied me. "Do you have ID with this name?" He pointed to my certification.

"Sure." I pulled out my passport and handed it over. He glanced at it and back to the PADI certifications then nodded. "Okay then, Kiki Hepburn. I see you have your own BCD."

I nodded, holding up the bag containing the black vest which would hold the air tank on my back and would inflate or deflate to allow me to rise or sink, called a Buoyancy Compensation Device, or BCD.

"How about weights? What do you usually use?"

"Eleven pounds."

He handed over a belt and stacked the small weights on the counter, which I then threaded onto the belt. These would weight me down so I could actually swim under water.

He smiled, a big open smile. "You can put your gear in the van outside. We're just waiting for a few more people."

I walked outside, where the younger man in a tank top was loading the last of the equipment. I admired the muscles of his back as he lifted the heavy air tanks. His shoulders tapered down to a trim waist and nice tight little—

He turned around, and to my horrible embarrassment, I realized it was the hot guy I had run into on the patio. He had taken off his island print shirt.

"Oh," I stammered, "look at this. Isn't this funny."

He raised his eyebrows and smirked. "Maybe you'll stick around long enough for me to find out your name this time."

My face warmed. "Kiki. I'm, uh, Kiki."

He smiled, the same beautiful white teeth as the man inside. "I'm Dex. Looks like we both have weird names."

"Oh." I looked down, straightening my sarong around my waist. "It's just a nickname."

"What's your real name?"

I looked out to the sea. "How far away is the dive location?"

He chuckled. "Five-minute drive to the dock, a half hour in the boat. I need to go grab the lunches. You can get in the van if you want."

I climbed in, picking the farthest back seat from where the two friendly men would be. I didn't need questions. I stuck in earbuds to avoid anyone talking to me and slid down into the seat, propping my knees along the top edge. Would I be able to fake my way through this day?

Some of the other divers had arrived and climbed in. There was a couple, apparently on their honeymoon, next to me on the back bench seat cuddling. The other was a lone man. He looked at me as he climbed in. Crap. Unless someone else alone showed up, he was going to end up being my dive partner. Part of me was hoping Dex would be my partner since underwater, no questions would be asked and I could look at his mostly naked, tanned body without it being weird. This man though, *ew*. Hair protruded from the top of his Aloha Lagoon T-shirt, escaping his ears, on his toes… This was going to be like diving with Sasquatch. To finish off the ick factor, he had a creepy tattoo of a snake winding up his arm.

Finally, the remaining divers arrived, the doors slammed shut, and we were off.

A few minutes into the drive, I squiggled up enough to be able to see the late arrivals. They were all women but appeared to be two separate groups, one a pair of middle-aged sisters (judging by their bickering) and the other what looked like a mother-daughter pair. When I inspected the latter closer, my heart just about stopped.

I could be wrong, and I hoped I was, but that sure looked like Claire D'Angelo. She was the gossipy best friend of Ainsley Rickenbacker. Maybe it wasn't though, as this girl had shorter dark hair, chopped in a fashionably haphazard style. But when her face turned to the side, her nose looked just like the one Claire got for her sixteenth birthday. As for the older woman, I hadn't seen her mother, Heather, in a few years either, but I knew she floated in the same patronizing volunteer circles as my mother. This woman looked very much like how I recalled Heather looking, from her waves of blonde hair to the hot pink pedicure and all the plastic surgery in between.

This could be very bad. What was I going to do if it was them? I couldn't very well pretend like I didn't see them when we would be on a boat together for most of the day. I decided to wait until Claire, if it was her, made the first move.

When we arrived at the dock, we lugged everything onto the boat, the *Mahina,* which had steps up the back and pads along the sides where we'd sit and flip down into the water. If you weren't careful about your flipping technique, you could bruise the back of your knees pretty good.

I had picked a reef tour because there would be a lot of sea life there, but I was really interested in seeing the lava tubes too. If this went well, maybe I could schedule another day. Well, once I had the little money problem figured out.

"All right," the older Hawaiian man said after we were all suited up and the tanks and hoses were all verified as okay. "You're all experienced, so you know to stay with your buddy. When your air gets low, come back for lunch and to decompress before the afternoon dive." He had already introduced himself and Dex as his son. "Dex will be suited up and diving to check on you occasionally or if you have any questions. I'll remain on the boat."

The two sisters had made a point of asking for Dex's help in fastening their gear and now fluttered their eyelashes at him. Dex just smiled and soaked up the attention. The pair that resembled Claire and her mother checked each other's equipment, leaving me wondering wistfully if my mother would ever do something like this with me.

I strained to hear their voices. The snooty accents, the

disdainful looks thrown at the middle-aged sisters, the complete lack of acknowledgement of me... All evidence pointed to them being my former classmate and her mother.

My dive partner didn't make any effort to talk, which was fine by me. I wasn't here to make friends, especially with a hirsute older man.

But he was watching me closely.

*　*　*

Hovering, suspended in the water, I watched a group of butterflyfish, mostly yellow with a black band near their tails, pass by. My dive partner and I had already investigated the coral and seen a rainbow of fish darting among it. I was trying hard to remember what they looked like so I could look them up later, but he was taking pictures. I didn't believe in that—why would I want to look through a lens at this, instead of looking at it directly? Live in the now, not take pictures to "experience" later.

I glanced up and blew air out of my regulator—the breathing apparatus in my mouth—watching the little silver balls sparkle their way to the water's surface. It looked like silver from here too, undulating and dancing thirty feet or so above us.

I was unsure what my favorite part of diving was—the amazement at the sheer number and variety of life under the sea or the feeling of calm it gave me. It was so quiet you could hear your heart beat between your inhales and bubbly exhales. I could feel my heart rate slowing to a more reasonable rate. I was sure now the other women were Claire and her mother, but I didn't have to think about that during my time submerged. This was my time.

My Sasquatchian dive partner gestured at me, rubbing his palm with the first two fingers of his other hand. He was asking me how my air supply was. I checked my gauge, put my fist in front of my chest to indicate it was getting low, and pointed at him. He nodded then pointed his thumbs upward, so we rose to the surface. When we popped out on top of the water and located the boat, we took our regulators out, pulled our face masks down, and kicked the rest of the way over on the surface. Once we got to the boat, he gestured for me to mount the ladder to get back on board first. I hoped he wasn't going to look at my butt but still pulled the fins off my feet and threw them on the *Mahina* before clambering up the ladder.

Once onboard, Kahiau unhooked our spent tanks and attached new ones while we ate underwhelming sandwiches with a thick and salty bologna-like meat. Dive operations were usually not very fancy, their money spent on more important things like safety, I supposed. But I didn't mind. I wasn't here for the food. I was here for the feeling I got when I was floating underwater. As far as I was concerned, it was the best thing in the world.

My good vibes deflated a little when Claire and her mother emerged from the sea like glowing mermaid goddesses. Looked like they both had more work done than just their noses, as Claire was definitely filling out her bikini top a bit more than I remembered.

Claire's appearance was a little startling, but it wasn't the bikini. She and Ainsley used to be clones—curvy with long blonde hair, though Claire was a bit shorter. The biggest difference in their appearance was Ainsley usually had a vapid air about her, while Claire's was more sullen. The new hair suited her and her attitude. And, I had to admit, went well with her petite frame.

Once they had their equipment off and their sandwiches in hand, they sat on the bench across from me. Claire and I made eye contact for the first time, and at that point, it would have been just downright rude not to acknowledge each other. Social graces were part of our DNA.

"Claire? That *is* you, isn't it? I thought it was! How long's it been?" I gushed.

She frowned slightly, and she and her mother exchanged a look. "Hey, Katherine. Maybe five, six years?"

Her mother smiled, and with it, the image of a shark popped into my head. "Katherine, I'm Heather. Remember me? How are you? What brings you to Aloha Lagoon?"

Hum. What to say now... "I remember our senior trip here and was looking for somewhere to dive." That should work. "Did I see Ainsley earlier? She's here too?"

Heather's smile froze and her eyes narrowed, making her

look downright dangerous. But there was still politeness to deal with. "Yes," she said through tight lips.

"Heather, what is this stuff?" Claire pointed at the pink meat in her sandwich.

Oh yeah. Her mother was one of those parents who wanted to be called by their first name by their own children as well as their children's friends. Either trying to connect with them as humans or not wanting to feel old. Probably the latter in Heather's case. (My mother? *Mrs. Barrington.*)

"I'm not sure." Heather poked at it, then sniffed it. "I don't have a clue, but I'm sure it's not on my diet." She dropped it on the bench next to her dismissively, then looked back at me. "Diving, huh? And how are your parents?"

The back of my neck prickled. "They're fine. Busy as always." I paused, considering how to word what I wanted to say. "Do you talk to them much?"

Her lips curved into her dangerous smile-like movement again. "Just a few weeks ago."

"Oh." *Dang it.* "If you talk to them again in the next few days, you don't need to mention you saw me here. Is that okay?"

She laughed without any hint of actual mirth. "Sure, honey. But only if you don't tell mine where I am." She gave me an exaggerated wink.

Well, okay then.

I started to say something mindless to Claire, but she abruptly got up and went over to Dex, running her hand down his arm to get his attention. At the same time, my dive partner sidled over and sat on the bench next to me. "Hey, I'm Joey." His New York accent was thick.

Immediately, my defenses went up. What were the odds of yet another New Yorker happening to be on this diving trip with me?

Still, I nodded to him and swallowed. "Kiki."

That seemed to amuse him. "Kiki?" He smirked. "Your name is *Kiki.*" He didn't say it like a question.

I was glad when the two sisters made their arrival back to the boat, fussing about the weight of their tanks and the awkwardness of the fins on their feet as they climbed the ladder. I was hoping they would distract this man, Joey, from talking to me. They were more his age, anyway.

But no dice.

"So, where you from, *Kiki*?" He chuckled again as he bit his sandwich.

"I'm on vacation to get away from it." I laughed unconvincingly.

He frowned before taking another bite of his sandwich. He chewed for a long time, watching the sisters, who were now fussing about their food. He turned his attention back to me abruptly. "So, you're from New York?"

My stomach dropped. "I'm on vacation," I squeaked.

"Vacation." He looked out over the sparkling water. "That's not what your parents are calling it."

CHAPTER TWO

———

All the air rushed out of my lungs. It felt like the time my regulator had malfunctioned when I was working on my deep diving certification thirty-five feet under the water with no air. Luckily I'd remembered the signal for "no air," and the instructor shared his regulator with me as we rose to the surface.

"I need to, um…" I dropped everything and jumped overboard like an insane fool. I dog-paddled to the other side of the boat for "privacy" and tried not to hyperventilate.

How did he find me? What was he going to do? Who exactly was he?

"Everything okay?" Dex's deep voice startled me, and I gasped.

I swung around to look at him. "No," I admitted, treading water.

His eyebrows furrowed. "What's wrong? Is your dive partner being a creep?"

I stared at him. "Why would you assume that?"

He shrugged, I thought. It was hard to tell with him treading water. "He's got a creepy vibe. Plus, an older dude diving with a pretty young lady…it was a lucky guess."

I grimaced. *That would work.* "Yeah, I don't really want to dive with him again. I'll just sit out the next one." *He thinks I'm pretty?*

He nodded. "We can reimburse you, or you can come again another day if you're going to be around a few more days." His eyebrows arched expectantly.

I nodded. "Yeah, that'd be great. I'd like to see the lava tubes, anyway."

The plan settled, he gestured to the boat. "You need to come back on though. We don't want to worry about you out here without gear."

I got back on the boat but sat as far away from Joey as I could and faced my body away from him. I heard Dex telling him I wasn't feeling well and he'd do the next dive with him. I put my head on the edge of the boat to give proof of my not feeling well, and I heard Joey's sarcastic laugh. And, unless I was imagining things, Heather's laugh too.

I watched as they geared back up to dive again. Dex said something to his dad about there being sea urchins, giving him a significant look. Kahiau grimaced and shook his head.

Once everyone was off the boat, Kahiau came over to me. "Sorry to hear your partner didn't work out. Dex says you're interested in seeing the lava tubes. We go there the day after tomorrow."

I nodded. "Is sea urchin code for a creepy dive partner?"

He laughed. "Yup. Happens more often than we want to admit."

We settled into an easy conversation about diving and living in Aloha Lagoon. The rest of the afternoon passed quickly, me helping out around the boat and listening to his stories about some of the crazy personalities that came on his dive trips.

The sun was lowering as we arrived back at the docks. I had managed to stay away from Joey, but once we were back at the dive shop and disembarking from the van, he blocked my way.

"We'll be getting on a plane tomorrow night, *Kiki*. I'll settle your bill with the resort tonight. Then you're coming with me."

"No," I said haughtily. "I'm diving again the day after tomorrow, and I can't fly for twenty-four hours after."

"*No*, you're not. It took me too long to find you as you traipsed around the world diving. You'll meet me in the café at ten a.m. and will stay with me until we get on the plane." He glared at me. "In case it isn't obvious, I was sent to find you and take you home. You'll be going with me."

My eyes stung with tears, which seemed to make him angry.

"That won't work on me, you little brat," he sneered. "See you in the morning. Or else."

I didn't want to know what "or else" meant.

* * *

I sat at the bar, drowning my sorrows. If Joey Sasquatch was going to pick up the tab, I might as well get the most out of it.

Casey, the bartender, rubbed a cloth on the bar and watched me. I guessed I was interesting to watch, over here, literally crying into a Mai Tai. When his girlfriend Samantha showed up, he said something to her, looking my way.

So, not surprisingly, the little Aussie appeared at my elbow. "Hi again. Want some company?"

"Not really."

"Well," she said slowly. "Casey asked me to sit with you. Seems there's a creepy guy in the corner who hasn't taken his eyes off you all night."

I didn't have to look to know exactly where he was. He had already raised his glass to me in greeting, followed by the two fingers pointed at his eyes then pointed at me gesture. He was letting me know he was watching me.

"Hairy guy?" I asked as Casey moved down the bar to us.

"Yeah." Casey polished the bar in front of us. "You know him?"

"Not really, or at least I don't want to know him." I released a sigh and rolled my head to release tension from my neck.

"Is he the guy from your dive trip today?" Casey asked.

I stared at him. "How'd you…?"

Casey laughed and tipped his head to the other end of the bar. Dex raised a beer to me.

"To be honest, Casey noticed him in here watching you last night, too. And I saw him follow you this morning when you went to the dive shop." She blushed. "Or at least I saw you walk past and then he did." Samantha reached a hand out and placed it on my arm. "You really don't know him?"

I shook my head and took a deep, shuddering breath.

Samantha and Casey had some sort of eye conversation.

Then Samantha turned to me. "Do you want to come stay at my house tonight? Well, my mom's house. My brother will be there too, and we'll watch out for you."

Could it be that easy? I could hide there for a while then sneak off into the night, never to be seen again by any of them.

Except…

"I have no money," I muttered.

Samantha's face scrunched up. "I wouldn't dream of you paying to stay."

I shook my head, making myself dizzy. "I mean to hide. I have no money without him."

Samantha and Casey exchanged another look, obviously confused.

"Then you do know him?" Casey said.

"No," I hissed, suddenly angry, "but I know who sent him." I stabbed a drunken finger in the air.

"Okay." Casey slid my Mai Tai away and replaced it with a water. "I think you've had more than enough for tonight."

"You're adorable," I laughed. I looked at Samantha. "He's adorable."

She gave me a tight smile. "I think so too."

"But that Dex guy, he's *hot*!" I said way too loudly.

She laughed and held a finger in front of her lips. I copied her movement.

"Come sit with me and my friends." She gestured toward a table outside.

I shrugged. "Sure." Let the weird night keep getting weirder.

But actually, I ended up having a nice time. Samantha's brother, Luke, was there, as well as her best friend, Alani. They were hilarious, and I forgot my troubles for a while. They joked and laughed together, no jealousy or cattiness. Just happiness. Nothing like my old schoolmates, where every word had a motive.

"Why so quiet?" Alani asked.

"I'm just enjoying listening to you all. You're so happy. Everyone here's so happy."

"You're not happy at your home?" Samantha's simple question was unknowingly very complex.

I looked away, trying to figure an answer.

"So, where are you from, Kiki?" Luke had his arm draped casually over the back of Alani's chair.

"I wish I was from here," I said, pulling a shank of my hair forward to wind around my fingers. "You guys are so lucky to live here."

"Why don't you stay, then?"

"Oh, I'd love to. But I'm out of money."

"Seems to me," said Luke, "you're old enough to get a job and find a place to stay. Only one life to live and all that."

I stared into my water with lemon. "I'm not really qualified to do anything." I scoffed at myself. "Twenty-two and nothing worth putting on a résumé."

Samantha laughed. "Of course you're qualified for something. You've done a lot of diving, right?" She put a hand on my arm. "When I came here, I got a job as a surf instructor because I love to surf."

I shook my head. "Well, I can't just be a scuba instructor. You have to get qualified by PADI for that." I squinted at the string of lights above me. "I'm not even sure they do instruction here, at least not for tourists. Certification just to dive takes a few days."

"PADI?" Samantha asked.

"The Professional Association for Diving Instructors. They certify the instructors as well as set standards for diver certification."

"Besides"—Alani waved a hand—"Jamie Parker is a dive instructor here at the resort. But you could ask her about how to get certified to instruct. Have you met her yet?"

I shook my head. "No, I decided to go to the Aloha Lagoon dive shop. I didn't realize there was another."

"It's part of Gabby's Island Adventures. But Jamie also works at the Happy Hula Boutique. You may have seen her there? She's the one with the real pretty eyes."

"Well, then, not instructing," Samantha interrupted. "Maybe leading excursions."

I laughed. "I don't know my way around here. And where exactly would I be doing this?"

Samantha rolled her eyes. "Gabby's? Or Aloha Lagoon

Diving?"

I stared at her.

"They're down an employee after one left." She shrugged. "Never hurts to ask. Plus"—she winked—"you could work with Dex."

My face warmed as I remembered what I practically screamed about him earlier. Casey switching me to water was a good move. "I can't afford the room at the resort on whatever a dive shop pays. Probably."

"We can help you find a place to live," Alani said. "Don't make excuses."

"You're an adult. You can do whatever you want." Samantha folded her arms, content with her plan for me.

It *was* a good plan. It might even help with my familial relations. But I could hear my father's voice telling me it wasn't reasonable. His voice also told me not to think I had a choice. Getting a job and staying would be adventurous and romantic, but I doubted Joey would give me a chance to find out. He was going to make me get on the plane with him. Maybe I could give him the slip at the airport?

I sighed and shook my head. I would just have to go home and face the music. "You don't understand."

"Well," said Samantha. "Explain it."

I shook my head. "Too long of a story."

She stared at me for a few moments and opened her mouth to say something further but was interrupted.

"Hey, can I sit with you guys?" Dex's deep voice was right above my head.

Everyone agreed, so he pulled over a chair and squeezed between Samantha and me, our elbows touching. I tried to shift so as to not feel like I was leaning against him. I snuck a glance and saw his dark eyes dancing with quiet laughter. "What?"

He shook his head then turned to Luke, and they started talking about fishing or something. I didn't know what he was saying. I was just listening to the soothing rumble of his voice. Soon my head snapped back up. I was falling asleep right here at the table!

"Obviously, we're very stimulating company," Alani laughed. "Why don't you head to bed?"

My face warmed. I agreed.

"I'll walk you." Dex rose and took hold of the back of my chair to help me up.

"I don't need an escort to my room." I stood and wobbled a bit on my heels. "It's not far."

"Sure you don't."

My face burned, and I hoped the darkness covered it. "If this is because of that Joey guy, he left the bar a long time ago."

"Oh, I know. I was keeping an eye on him." Dex stretched his arms above his head. "Aloha Lagoon is my home. I want you to feel safe here."

I slung my purse across my body, a move which would have horrified my mother. "Oh, he won't hurt me."

"How can you be so sure?"

"I just know." I glanced up at him.

We said our good nights to the others at the table and headed off toward my room.

I took his offered arm and let him lead me through the courtyard, past the gurgling fountain. I attempted to walk quietly since it was past midnight, but that was hard to do on cobblestones in four-inch Jimmy Choos without looking like a tightrope walker. (I have no idea how the Italians do it!) I was trying to go for sexy sashaying, but that wasn't happening. Especially when my heel got caught in the space between stones.

My ankle turned and I started to fall, but Dex reached out his other arm and caught me. He held me for longer than necessary, but man, did he smell good. His closeness was starting to make me tingle. His face inches from mine didn't help.

My goodness, his lips look soft.

Then those lips moved. "Are you in trouble?"

I laughed. "It's just the heels. My ankle hurts a little but—"

"I wasn't talking about your walking ability."

"Oh." I looked away as I took a step back. "Sort of."

"Anything I can help with?"

I looked back at him. Maybe bluntness was best. "I have no money and nowhere to go."

He studied me for a moment. "Hmm."

I faked a smile. "No worries. I'll figure something out." I turned to continue to my room, the little flash of a possibility of a Dex-fueled fantasy night dashed.

He didn't move. "Would your family help you out?"

My fake smile slipped away, and I started walking.

"Kiki?" He trailed behind.

"I can't ask. I'm an adult. I can do whatever I want," I said stubbornly, parroting what Samantha said earlier. I turned a corner and stopped so abruptly Dex grabbed my upper arms to keep us from colliding. We stood stock-still, listening to an *I'm trying to whisper but am really yelling* voice coming out of the darkness. There weren't many places around the resort that were dark, but these people had found a niche hidden from the fairy lights in the trees and the flaming tiki torches.

"You have to," a woman was saying. "Think of what this would do to Ainsley!"

A man's voice answered, clearly arguing, but both the pitch and volume were low enough that I couldn't understand him.

I suddenly became very conscious of Dex's body behind me, so close and yet not quite touching. Despite wanting to know more about this whispered argument about Ainsley, the feeling of him so close to me made me uncomfortable and desperate to get away. I shook off his arms and hurriedly continued down the passageway.

Once we got to my room, I unlocked the door and slipped inside. "Thanks for walking me. Good night."

CHAPTER THREE

———

I went to the patio for breakfast, fully expecting to see Joey there waiting for me. I sat until eleven, pretending to read and dreading his arrival, but he never came.

While I waited with my dread, I pondered the events of the past few days. It was strange my former classmates had shown up at the same place I was trying to hide out. Was it a coincidence they were here *and* Joey found me? Or did they lead him here somehow? Maybe someone saw me and called my parents, who dispatched him. I had only been here four days now but hadn't seen them until yesterday. Granted, I never left my room the first day I was here, spending it sleeping off my jet lag and ordering room service, but I was out exploring on day two. I hadn't asked Claire or Heather when they had arrived, but they didn't look jetlagged.

I grew impatient with waiting. I went to the front desk and asked if there were any messages for my room.

The young man at the front desk shook his head. "I'm sorry, no. Were you expecting one?"

I shook my head. "No, not really."

He tapped at his computer for a moment. "There is a note that your payment method was updated though."

"My payment method?"

"A new credit card was put on your account. Apparently the first card was denied."

Oh my gosh. He did pay my bills.

"Oh, of course." I waved a hand to make it seem like I had just forgotten. "Was the departure updated too?"

The clerk shook his head. "It wasn't closed out. Just a new card." He looked at me with chocolate-colored eyes. "Is there anything else I can help you with, Ms. Hepburn?"

I gave a quick shake of my head. In any other situation, I would've asked about who paid my bill, but I already knew the answer. I thanked the desk clerk and left. Maybe Joey slipped a note under my door giving me a new time to meet?

But there was nothing at the room, just my packed bags.

Confused but not unhappy with the turn of events, I went for a walk along the beach. So, lodging and food was taken care of, for the time being. But…it would verify they had found me. So, either I let myself be found, or I got the heck out of the resort and moved on.

With no money.

Or did I have money again?

Curious to see if my debit card had been refilled, I hurried back to the room and got it. I decided trying to use it at the resort wasn't the best idea, so I walked downtown to a grocery store and tried to buy a banana.

No dice.

And no banana. So, back at the resort, I went to lie on the beach for a while. When I got bored, I walked along the beach and ended up at the Aloha Lagoon Dive shop. I was surprised to see Kahiau there, talking with a policeman on the porch. I slid inside the shop and went to study the poster with fish of the Hawaiian reef to identify the ones I hadn't known yesterday.

"Good afternoon."

I jumped and spun around. Thankfully, it was Kahiau and not Dex.

"Oh, hi. Everything okay?" I gestured to where the policeman had been.

"We were broken into last night."

"Oh no!" *If they lost their money, there was no way I could ask for a job here.* I chided myself for my selfish thought. "Was it bad?"

He shook his head, his eyebrows knit together. "The thief only took diving weights."

"What?" I looked around the room. Of all the equipment, diving weights were a weird thing to steal. "Those aren't necessarily cheap, but they're kind of heavy to abscond with. And there's more expensive equipment."

He nodded. "That's what I was thinking. I debated even reporting it. They didn't even take all of them. Just enough to make us have to cancel today's dive."

"Oh." I frowned. Disappointment surged through me.

"Don't worry." He laughed. "Dex has gone to borrow more from Gabby's for tomorrow."

"Could someone have accidentally taken them home after the dive yesterday?"

He shook his head. "The officer asked too. But no. We account for everything after each dive. Sixty pounds of weights don't just get lost."

Considering the weights came in increments of ten and under, that was a lot of weights.

I looked around the shop. "No cameras?"

He laughed. "No, no cameras. Locks on the door are usually enough around here." He tipped his head at me. "So, are you still on for the lava tubes tomorrow? Dex was under the impression you were leaving today."

I smiled, my cheeks tight. "I thought I was too, but I may be around a few more days."

He nodded. "Good, good. See you tomorrow morning, then."

I hesitated on my way to the door. "Kahiau, my dive partner from the other day…he's not signed up for tomorrow, is he?"

Kahiau shook his head. "No. All ladies tomorrow."

"Great." I nodded and scooted on out of there.

* * *

I walked back to the resort along the beach, looking for shells to pick up in the surf. I was so engrossed I almost didn't notice a couple sitting on the sand about ten feet from me. Well, not a couple per se, since they were brother and sister.

Erg.

Claire quickly looked away when I raised my head, but her brother, Todd, was looking straight at me. He nudged Claire with an elbow, and she blew out a breath loud enough for me to hear as far away as I was. I raised a hand in greeting.

"Katherine," Todd said in a monotone. I had never been impressed with his brain, but the rest of him was nice to look at.

He was a lacrosse player (or "lax bro") back in the day and still wore his sandy brown hair in a modern mullet, like most lacrosse players did. Or at least did a few years ago. But it always kind of grossed me out that a girl could date her best friend's twin brother. Maybe because they didn't look like twins, Todd being a Ken doll lookalike and having a good foot on Claire. In fact, if they hadn't come from the same womb, I would think dark-haired Claire was adopted.

"Hey, Todd." I waved my hand again, then clamped it to my side, embarrassed. "How are you?" Now that I knew he was here, I was surprised he hadn't been diving with us yesterday. But when I got closer, I saw his face was pale, with red-rimmed eyes with Prada-sized bags under them. The dude looked sick or just very, very unhappy.

He snorted. "Just dandy."

My next words were based on an assumption, and you know what they say about assumptions…

"So, where's Ainsley?" I looked from face to face, surprised to see them contorting.

"Why would I know?" He suddenly stood, shaking off his sister's attempts to take his arm. "I couldn't care less where she is." And he stormed off down the beach, expletives floating back to me on the breeze.

"Oh…" I watched as he stomped away, then looked back down at Claire. She was glaring at me with a look that could kill.

"Really," she said through gritted teeth. "Did you really have to do that?"

I cringed. "What'd I do? What's wrong? Did they break up? I just assumed since I saw her…"

"Well, you assumed wrong. Very wrong." She got to her feet and into my personal space. "We are here for Ainsley's wedding."

"Wait." I took a step back. "To Todd?"

Claire's face flushed a shade of purple close to that of a flower I had seen earlier. "No!" she growled.

"Oh. That's…" What? Nice? Weird?

"That's *what*?!" Her eyebrows shot up to her hairline.

"Nice?" I'll go with that.

"No."

"No?" I tipped my head. "Not nice?"

"Definitely not." Claire bent to pick up a sweatshirt they had been sitting on and shook it as she stood. "Since she's marrying the man she cheated on Todd with."

* * *

"I see you're still here." Casey slid a Mai Tai across the bar to me.

"Surprise, surprise." I smiled. I was finally feeling a little more secure after no sign of Joey all day. *Maybe they called off their dog?* I laughed at that, Joey being so hairy and all.

"Anything to do with the creeper being gone?"

"What? No. Not really." I looked away, across the bar at a group of rowdy college-aged kids. "Why, have you seen him?"

"Neither hide nor hair, which is saying a lot." Casey laughed as he turned away to serve another customer.

I may have been feeling better about that situation but now was perplexed with this whole wedding situation. Todd was clearly angry about it—so why was he here? Why would he come over fifteen hours on a plane to watch his ex-girlfriend marry someone else?

"Katherine?! Is that you?" A woman's shrill voice was right behind me. A very familiar voice.

Oh no! I froze, not turning my head, despite my curiosity. Then a hand fell on my shoulder.

"Who is it?" This time, a male voice. Not as familiar.

The hand became an arm pulling me into a drunken hug. I had no choice but to turn and look at the couple leaning toward me, each holding a glass of champagne.

What the heck...

"Oh, as I live and breathe! Of all the little bars in all the world!" Ainsley shrieked, grabbing me in a hug and spilling champagne on my shoulder. "I haven't seen you in, what, three years?" She held me at arm's length, and her smile faltered. "You...you do remember me, don't you? It's Ainsley...from—"

"Of course I remember you, silly goose! I'm just so shocked to see you here! And..." I turned to the man and stared, dumbfounded. "Um...Mr. D'Angelo?"

The two shifted, looking around them uneasily, Ainsley flipping her long blonde locks over her shoulder.

"We, uh…we've…" Mr. D'Angelo looked at Ainsley. He scratched his sandy brown hair self-consciously, making me notice the touch of gray around his temples.

"We're engaged!" Ainsley held up her ring finger, and I was shocked she could manage to do so, with the size of the boulder on her slender finger.

I stared at her hand. This was awkward. Ainsley was engaged to marry Mr. D'Angelo. Her best friend's and ex-boyfriend's father. Their *father*! Ainsley was my age, and he was…father-aged. He looked good for his age, but still. I swallowed hard. This was a lot to wrap my head around.

I did my best Mrs. Barrington-of-the-Long Island-Barringtons imperious smile. "Congratulations! Shall we get a table and catch up?"

If "catching up" meant sitting and staring at our drinks between bouts of gushing about how nice the weather was here and *not* asking the *really interesting* questions, then we did a lot of catching up. I was left wondering how I hadn't heard a whisper about this super juicy gossip, and they did nothing to quell the curiosity, other than tell me they had been on the island for three days (same as me) and that the wedding was in a week. If there was one time I was tempted to call my mother, it was now. I guess this was the price I paid for not calling my mother more often.

Ned, as I was asked to call him, had ordered another bottle of champagne, and we raised our glasses in a toast. He looked at his much-younger bride. "What are we toasting to, sweetheart? Freedom?"

She pulled her glass away from her glossy lips mid-guzzle and giggled. She leaned into his arm, her chest spilling out of her top more than a little. (Which was an off the shoulder, flowered, and probably silk—and if I'm not mistaken, an Oscar de la Renta.) "Oh, yes. Freedom!" She raised her flute again and downed the remaining champagne in one gulp, then let go with a little ladylike burp. *Classy.*

All of his attention was fixed on her chest pressing into his arm. He didn't seem to even hear her tipsy response. "Yes," he murmured. "Beautiful freedom."

Ainsley giggled again, and her free hand went under the table. I looked away. So...icky! "Well," she purred. "Maybe we should go celebrate in another way."

Ned was practically drooling. "Yes, let's."

And without even a good night to me, they scurried off, hopefully to their room.

I shuddered. Ainsley had snagged a very rich man, which left me pondering about the original Mrs. D'Angelo. And the state of her friendship with his daughter. Neither Claire nor Heather made any indication of something being amiss on the boat yesterday. But this definitely explained why Todd was here, as well as his reaction to my innocent question. They were here to see their father remarry.

"Everything okay?"

I looked up.

Dex was standing there, beer in hand. "You look a little forlorn."

"No, not forlorn."

"Were those friends of yours?"

"I wouldn't call them that. Just some overly friendly people." I gestured at an abandoned chair, so he sat, moving the champagne glasses away.

"Mmm." He studied me. "You didn't seem too happy to be talking to them."

I shrugged. "Not exactly, no."

He tipped his head and continued to watch me. "So, you must've gotten your money issue sorted out?"

"Not really." I looked in his big brown eyes. I didn't even know him but hated feeling like I was lying to him. "It's a—"

"—long story," he finished for me.

My face warmed, and I looked away.

We sat in silence for what seemed like hours but was probably a few awkward minutes.

"Well, then, I guess I'll see you in the morning." Dex stood abruptly and walked away, the third person to leave me without a goodbye that night.

*　*　*

The morning came, well, early. I grabbed some coffee and pastries in the lobby as I hurried out, lugging my equipment bag. Nibbling the pastry as I hurried down the beach, I spilled the coffee on me several times. Good thing I'd be wearing this in the water.

Dex was all business, but his father greeted me warmly. I was the last to arrive, so the van pulled out as soon as I was on board.

As Kahiau had promised, all of the day's divers were women, two of them being the sisters from the first day. I noticed immediately we were an odd number. I put my hand over my eyes. I would be diving with Dex.

After we arrived at the site and dropped anchor, Kahiau suited up to dive with me, not Dex. I wasn't sure if it was relief or regret that washed over me.

"I want to make sure you see all the best parts," Kahiau said as we perched on the side of the boat.

"Awesome." I fitted my mask over my eyes then stuck my regulator in my mouth.

"Ladies first." He pointed with his thumb over his shoulder.

I leaned back until I did a backward roll, tumbling over into the water, making sure to lift my legs to avoid hurting the backs of them on the edge of the boat.

Once we were in the water, he led the way. I followed him toward the craggy, seaweed-covered rocks and then to an underwater arch. It was an eerie blue, not dark, but few fish were here.

We swam around under there, occasionally seeing the other divers. A sea turtle, my absolute fave thing to see, came paddling past us, his long flippers making him glide along. Another set of divers went by, so I waved and pointed at the turtle so they could experience it too.

But one of the divers was thrashing and jerking, clutching her regulator. Without stopping to think, I kicked over to her and grabbed her by her vest. Her eyes inside her mask were wild, and she gestured madly at her chest.

I pointed at my regulator and then to her, nodded, and waited for her to nod back. Taking a steadying breath, I took my regulator out of my mouth as she removed her own and put mine in her mouth. I held my breath while she took two jagged breaths, coughing. She took one more, slower, and then passed the regulator back to me. After two breaths, I passed it back then looked around for Kahiau.

The woman's dive partner had gone to fetch him, and he was just turning around. I took my next two breaths then gestured upward with my thumb like a hitchhiker, holding it above my head where everyone could see it. We began to rise to the surface, continuing to alternate breaths, or "buddy breathe."

Once we popped out on the surface, we both kept holding each other, coughing, and gasping for air. "Are you okay?" I pulled my mask down under my chin and wiped my hair back. I looked around to get my bearings as Kahiau and the other diver surfaced next to us. Together, we paddled toward the boat, Kahiau helping the diver with the bad regulator up first then me.

Once we were on board, the woman grabbed me in an awkward hug. "You saved my life!"

I patted her back awkwardly, aware Dex was standing there watching, confused.

"What happened?" He helped the woman out of her BCD vest.

"I don't know," she gasped. "I just couldn't get air anymore for some reason. I thought I was going to die." She looked over at me. "Then she came and shared her air."

Kahiau patted me on the shoulder, beaming. "She did an amazing job."

While we ate lunch and sunned, the father and son checked the diver's malfunctioning equipment.

"It looks like this O-ring might be the problem." Dex held his hand out to his father.

Kahiau took it, inspected it, nodded, and handed it back.

The diver was surprisingly cool about it all, now that her shaking had stopped. But even though they had spare equipment, she passed on the second dive, so, after our break I was paired with her friend.

Together we descended into the crystal-clear water and headed for the lava rock formations again. Dex trailed behind, keeping an eye on us and the other pair.

My new dive partner was the grabby, excitable type. She grabbed my arm when a zebra-striped moray eel slipped from behind one rock to another, when a turkey fish ventured close, and when a silver needlefish floated by. So, I wasn't surprised when she grabbed me again.

But this time, it was no fish. She was pointing at something in the distance and raised her hand like she was shrugging. Figuring she was saying she wanted to go see what it was, I gestured for her to lead the way. I was distracted by a flounder shuffling into the sand when she screamed. Well, as much as you could underwater with your mouth full of a regulator.

She grabbed my arm again, pointing and making noises. I assumed it was a barracuda or a shark. But it *so* wasn't.

It was a man, arms and legs floating upward, attached to the sea floor somehow. There was a black garbage bag tied over his head, so I couldn't see the face. But I knew exactly who it was.

The dead man was very hairy, with a snake tattoo slithering up his arm.

CHAPTER FOUR

———

I tried to calm my dive partner. When I looked around, Dex was nowhere to be seen. So I signaled to her we should rise to the surface there. It did occur to me on our ascent that perhaps we could just *not* report the body. My problem was gone. Maybe if we just didn't mention it…

But that didn't happen. As soon as we reached the surface, my dive partner put her mask on top of her head and started shouting, waving her arms. Kahiau and the boat were a good distance away, and he couldn't very well start the engine with divers in the water.

Dex popped up a few feet from us then swam over. "What's wrong? Please don't tell me there's another equipment issue."

"No," screamed my dive partner, even though he was only a few feet from her. "There's a body, like, a dead body!"

He stared at her. "A…human?"

I couldn't help but snort-laugh. "I don't think she'd get so frantic over a dead fish."

He looked my way. "You saw it too?"

I nodded. "I think I recognize who it is, too." I gestured down. "You should go see."

He nodded and descended. A few minutes later, he came back to the surface. He raised his arms in the air, forming an O. At that signal, Kahiau started to pull up his anchor. Dex and I both descended a few feet to look for the other divers, and when we spotted them, Dex pointed at me, then them. I nodded and started swimming to where they were. I needed to let them know the boat was moving and not to go near the surface.

After the anchor was dropped again, I headed up to the boat with the other divers. Air and time were running out anyhow.

The other divers were excited to hear the morbid news, but soon the boat became somber. Dex and his father stood together and spoke quietly to each other. They had called in the emergency, and now we waited.

I sidled up to them and looked at Dex. "You think it's him, right?"

He frowned but nodded. "Yeah. That tattoo…"

I looked between them. "It didn't exactly look like an accident."

"With a plastic bag wrapped around his head? Um, no." Dex shook his head.

Kahiau looked worried. "No, and now I'm worried we just found our stolen weights."

We were finally allowed to depart after the Coast Guard arrived. When I was questioned about whether or not I knew him, I was tempted again to say I didn't.

Because I didn't really *know* him, did I.

I ended up admitting he was my dive partner two days ago but left out the part about him watching me and talking to me. I didn't want to get involved with this.

Then it occurred to me, when I was sitting on the edge of the boat as it headed back to the dock. The police might find the connection between the dead man and me when they talked to the resort. They might be able to tell he paid for my room. I needed to get out of it. Like, now.

Dex came over to check on me. "You doing okay?"

I took a deep breath and let it out slowly. "Yeah. This has been some day."

He nodded. He sat with me the rest of the trip to the dock. I tried to enjoy the sun, but he was watching me.

When we got back to the dive shop, I lingered, helping them unload, putting off going back to the resort.

"You did good out there," Kahiau said. "I'm impressed."

I smiled and looked at my feet. "Thanks. Anyone would have done it." I looked back up at him.

He raised his eyebrows. "One would hope, but trust me when I say that might not be the case. You were very calm under pressure. Not once, but twice." He watched me for a moment.

"Dex thinks you might be looking for a job. I might have one for you."

I stared at him. "Really?"

He nodded. "And I have an idea of a place to stay. Wouldn't be all fancy like the resort, but it would be affordable for someone with no money."

My eyes began to water. "Really?"

His smile grew wide. "We can consider this morning your interview. You're hired!"

I bounced on my heels. "Oh, wow, thank you!"

He laughed. "I'll have Dex take you over to the house that has a room for rent."

Dex appeared from behind his father. "I'll take her where?"

"Auntie Akamai's. See if the room is okay for her."

Dex stared at his father and then me. "Really?" He looked doubtful but carried my bag to a jeep and offered me a hand to get in. I rolled my eyes but accepted it.

Dex spun the tires as we pulled out of the small dirt lot. He shot a look at me. "Dad said he was going to offer you a job."

I nodded. "He did. And I accepted!"

"Good." He snuck a peek at me. "Just out of curiosity, have you ever had a job before?"

"Um…no. But…" I watched the scenery pass and searched for what to say. I was a hard worker? I learned quickly? I graduated college with a 3.8 GPA? Liked fish?

"I'm glad you accepted and are being the whole *adult doing what you want* thing. But"—he shot me a look—"I'm not sure you fully understand what it entails."

A stab of anger shot through me. "Why? You think I'm stupid? A child?"

"No," he laughed. "I think you haven't seen the room for rent yet." Just as he said that, we pulled up in front of a bungalow-type house surrounded by palm trees and flanked by hibiscus and bird-of-paradise plants. The ocean was visible just beyond the house.

"Oh, it's lovely!" I gushed.

Dex barked out a laugh and got out of the jeep. He came around to open my door, but I had already hopped out.

A Hawaiian woman filled the doorway of the bungalow as we approached. Wearing a garish flower-print muumuu, she looked like she had never had a bad day, her smile was so wide.

"Dex, my *keiki*! Come give Auntie a hug!" She pulled him into her arms before she even finished the words. Then she turned to me. "Oh, your friend, she is lovely!" And she came at me with open arms.

Eeek. I let her hug me, tentatively patting her back. A shriek from inside the house made me jump.

Auntie Akamai chuckled at my reaction. "No worries, it's just my parrot." She turned and bellowed into the house, "*Paulie*!"

"You have a parrot?" I tried to keep my mouth from hanging open. "Named Polly?"

"Yes." She smiled, holding out an arm. "He's Paulie, P-A-U-L-I-E, not Polly like a girl parrot." As she finished her sentence, a flash of color came flying at us, and I instinctively ducked.

Auntie Akamai hooted again. "He won't hurt you. You can pet him if you like."

I straightened and faced the bird, nose to beak. I'd never been too keen on birds, but he was lovely. His feathers were a deep gray, and when he turned to the side, I could see red on his tail feathers. His eyes though…they were unsettling. White with little black pupils, like how a child would color eyes in. I tried not to shudder as I tentatively reached out a hand and touched a feather for a millisecond.

Auntie Akamai snorted and put the bird on her shoulder. "She'll get used to you, sweetums," she said to the bird, who responded by giving the creepiest laugh I've ever heard. Then she turned to me. "Come," she gushed, "I'll show you the room."

But instead of walking into the house, she led us around the side of it. And there, under a massive Banyan tree, was what looked like a small garage, but with three walls of screen between vertical boards. She unlocked a knob on the wooden screened door and, stepping through the doorway, gestured her arm to encompass the room. *Ah.* This was why Dex was doubtful.

Cement floor. Walls of screens, no glass. A tiny twin

bed with a metal frame, not much more than a cot pushed up against the one solid wall. A small table with a single chair. A hanging fan with a light attached to one of the ribs of the ceiling. A tiny two-burner cookstove, microwave, and refrigerator. An even smaller bathroom.

It was much, much smaller than the pool house at home. *My mother would be horrified.*

"I'll take it."

"Yes?" Auntie Akamai beamed at me.

I looked around. Well, it had a bed and a toilet (with actual walls around it). I didn't have much use for a kitchen since I didn't know how to cook, and the sea breeze blew in through the screens. And it was clean.

"Yes! It is the perfect hideaway." I beamed at my new landlord.

Dex looked shocked, but Auntie Akamai was over the moon. "Ha! A hideaway! I love it. Now, we won't worry about the whole first and last months' rent deal part for now, but once you make some money working for Kahiau, we can work it out. How's that sound?"

I had no idea what apartments went for, let alone screen-encased shacks. "Okay," I stammered, uncomfortable by the kindness and generosity.

She dug a key out of a deep pocket on her voluminous dress and handed it over after another smothering hug.

"Do you need help moving your things over?" Dex found his voice again.

"Ah…sure, thank you," I said.

We went back to the resort, and I hurriedly packed my things not already in a suitcase. Dex took my bags back to the jeep, laboring like a packhorse (but barely breathing heavy), and I went to the front desk.

"I need to check out. I'm moving on." I gave the clerk my room number.

He tapped at the computer keys for a moment. "Okay, Miss Hepburn, you're good to go. Have a good journey. *Aloha.*"

I hurried out to the jeep and jumped in. "All right, let's go!"

He smiled over at me. "You seem happy."

I thought about that as I buckled my seat belt. "I guess I am. I'm excited. I'm off on an adventure."

He gave me a weird look but chuckled as we pulled out of the driveway for the short drive back to Auntie Akamai's. Dex carried all my suitcases in, not even breaking a sweat. He showed me the closet—a cabinet with a curtain hanging on the front. I hadn't noticed it before and had to admit I may have recoiled in disgust at the mangled wire hangers on the pole. Well, I wouldn't be hanging the Dior on any of *those*. Mr. Dior would spin in his grave if I even considered it.

By nightfall I was settled in the small room, having left my fancier clothes in the suitcase I had slid under the twin bed. I locked the flimsy door and climbed between the sheets, exhausted by the activity and stress of the day.

I slept surprisingly well and woke with the sunrise streaming through the, um, walls. The sounds of crashing waves and birds filled the air, and I went to look out one of the windows.

This was a true paradise.

I threw open the door and ran down to the beach like a child, dancing around the edge and getting wet up to my ankles. I could definitely live with this.

I spotted some people walking toward me on the beach and realized I was still in my nightgown, so I hurried back to the house. I tried the tiny shower out, using the resort soaps I had taken. No hairdryer, which was okay. It would just be getting wet again, so I twisted it into a knot on the back of my head.

"Helloooo!" called a voice.

"Hello!" shrieked another.

I whipped around to see Auntie Akamai at the door, a bamboo tray in her hands and Paulie on her shoulder.

"Oh, good morning." I held open the door for her, and she slid through sideways.

"I made you breakfast. You need to eat hearty to deal with those two all day!" She put the tray on the tiny table and gestured at it. "Eat."

I stared at the tray. It held more food than I ate in a day, certainly not at a single meal. Eggs, bacon, potatoes, sausage, toast, rolls, rice, fruits, a yogurt, a glass of milk, and a coffee. It was a virtual smorgasbord.

"Oh wow, you didn't have to feed me," I said.

"Oh, it's included. And you could use a little meat on your bones." She stared pointedly at my hips. Or at least where womanly hips would have been had I possessed them.

I realized, as my face warmed, I was wrapped in a towel, but she behaved like I had proper clothes on.

"Meat on your bones!" squawked the parrot.

I laughed. "And good morning to you too, Paulie."

"Paulie want a cracker?" Paulie squawked at me before leaning his head against Auntie Akamai's cheek, where he crooned, "Cracker."

"Yes, lovie, I'll get you a cracker." She looked at me. "Did you sleep okay?"

I nodded. "The sound of the waves is very soothing. I slept like a baby."

She smiled, pleased. "Well, I'll let you get to it." She glanced at the sun. "Dex will be by to get the sandwiches for today's tour in about twenty minutes. I need to get them made." She turned to go then paused. "Oh, by the way, there's an old bike outside if you need to get around anywhere. You're welcome to use it."

Oh goodness. I hadn't even thought of transportation, and I hadn't ridden a bike—or at least one which wasn't fixed to a spot in a room full of my fellow panting spandex-clad gerbils—in close to...never. I didn't exactly have the typical childhood.

But at least I had a ride to work today, as Dex had said he'd be back in the morning to get me and apparently the sandwiches as well.

I had hung my few "casual" items on the wire hangers in the closet or had them folded on the shelf above the bar. I pulled out a pair of shorts. If I was working and not just diving, I probably should wear normal clothes, not a sarong. I had brought multiple dive-appropriate swimsuits, but if this was going to be my job, I was probably going to need more. I picked one out and put it on, throwing a T-shirt and the shorts over it.

I ate as much as I could manage then put the leftovers in the mini fridge, right as Dex's jeep was pulling in. I looked around the room and wondered if my more expensive items of clothing would be secure here. Being that the windows and walls were screens, perhaps it was a silly thing to worry about. Of course they weren't. But this was a tropical paradise! Did they even have crime here?

So, off I went on my adventure in adulting, excited and certainly not expecting what was coming next.

CHAPTER FIVE

———

What came next was getting grilled by the Five-O.

We pulled up and parked in the shade of a large leafy tree. I carried the box of sandwiches and chips while he carried our bags. As soon as we came around the edge of the shop, we saw a tall man in a Hawaiian shirt standing on the porch alongside Kahiau. The stranger was holding the dive shop logbook in one hand while the other pointed at it. Both of their heads popped up when they heard us approaching.

"Hi kids." Kahiau waved us up to join them. "This is Detective Ray. He needs to ask us some questions."

Oh drat.

Dex dropped our bags at the bottom of the stairs, and I set the box on the step, following him up. I glanced up at him and was surprised to see a scowl on his handsome face.

The detective, on the other hand, was all smiles. He greeted Dex and shook my hand, restating his name as Ray Kahoalani. He then turned his brown eyes on me. "You are the young lady who found the body?"

I shuddered, then nodded. "The other girl saw him first but pointed him out to me."

He nodded. "Yes, I've already spoken to her. She made it sound like you knew him, or thought you might."

Double drat.

I looked at Kahiau, and he just smiled at me. *Why does everyone smile so much here?!* It was endearing and engaging at first, but at this moment it was downright annoying. Kind of like those feral chickens wandering around everywhere.

I looked back to the detective and raised my chin, trying to once again channel my mother. "We were both partnerless on arrival, so we had to be dive partners."

Detective Ray's face was like stone. "And?"

"That's all. I'd never seen him before then."

"Kahiau said you didn't do a second dive with him." The detective had a kind face and looked like a big pushover, with an attitude that he couldn't care less about any of this.

I schooled my face to remain calm and impassive. The last thing I needed to do was react. Pretty much in any way. So I shrugged. "He gave me a bad vibe."

All three men just stood, and the silence drew out until the detective finally spoke again. "I was under the impression he said or did something inappropriate? A..." He looked at Kahiau and raised his eyebrows. "Sea urchin?"

Dex had been standing, his head swiveling back and forth between the detective and me. Now Detective Ray turned to him. "Were you aware of anything going wrong?"

Dex scowled. "The clients were eating lunch and talking. I don't eavesdrop, so I don't know what was said, but Kiki said she didn't want to dive with him again. She has every right to not want to dive with someone she's not comfortable with. You are trusting the other person with your life."

The detective turned back at me. "So there were no unwelcomed advances?"

Before I could stop myself I blurted out, "Gross! No!" I slapped my hand over my mouth. Took a calming breath. "He did not do or say anything inappropriate. I just didn't want to dive with him."

"Can we get to work now? We have a dive scheduled to leave in less than ten minutes. We have a lot of work to do." Dex gestured between us, and I was glad he included me in the gesture but was confused by his attitude with the detective.

Detective Ray shrugged. "Sure." He held a hand out to stop me though. "One last question. What is your name?"

I plastered on a big fake smile, making those years with braces worth it. "Kiki Hepburn."

I followed Dex inside but just stood in the middle of the store, unsure of what to do. Dex picked up an air tank in each hand and lugged them out the door.

Then a thought paralyzed me.

The logbook was in the detective's hand. The logbook

which would most likely show my certification information, as well as *my real name.*

He would know I lied.

Was it illegal to lie to the police?

Kahiau came in, and I was jerked out of my mini panic attack. "Can you help me check everyone in?" He gestured toward the door as a couple walked in.

I walked robotically to behind the counter with him and stood next to him. He slid the logbook in front of me and handed me a pen. "I'll check while you record."

I numbly did as I was told, writing in each diver's name, where they were staying, and an emergency contact. Halfway through the third diver, I realized what I was writing.

Crapola.

Not only did Detective Ray see my real name, but also my parents' names and a phone number.

Once the clients and Kahiau went to get equipment fitted, I flipped the page over to the previous one. Sure enough, there it was. *Katherine T. Barrington, Long Island, NY.* With *Kiki Hepburn* written small and in parenthesis in the margin. Following my name were my parents' names and my mother's cell phone number.

"Kiki. Earth to Kiki!" Dex was suddenly there, scowling at me. "Wake up."

I jumped, flipping the page back. "What? Yeah. Okay."

"Grab the sandwiches and get in the van."

My eyes widened.

Dex softened. "Please."

But his softness didn't last. He was polite to the divers, but was slamming things around, scowling at nothing. He didn't hide that he was upset about something. He had seemed fine on the drive here, if not aloof again, so it must have been the detective. He hadn't seemed upset with the Coast Guard when they questioned him when the body was found. Why was he upset now?

Once the divers were all out of the boat, Kahiau called me over to the boat steering area. He asked if I knew how to drive a boat, and I shook my head, embarrassed to admit to him that we had staff that piloted my parents' yacht. I used to sit and watch when I was small, but certainly had never driven one before. I wouldn't have been allowed to and never dreamed of asking. I had no reason to need to know how to.

He gave me the basics in case I ever needed to know during an emergency, obviously thinking I knew how to drive a car. I never had a need to get a license in the city…and in high school had a driver at the ready.

I looked out over the cerulean blue water with its tiny whitecaps. He was assuming I'd still be here. I thought I would be too, but this Detective Ray might change that.

When we were done with the impromptu boat-driving lesson, it was time for the divers to emerge from the sea. I busied myself with helping people out of their gear and handing out lunches. Once everyone was settled, I grabbed a sandwich myself and perched on the boat's edge. I couldn't believe how hungry I was after my massive breakfast. This must be what it feels like when you work. *I feel so lame.*

Dex wandered over and leaned against the side of the boat. "How's your first day going?"

"Getting better," I said, then realized it sounded like I was saying him coming to sit with me was making it better. "Um, so what is this stuff in the sandwiches?" I winced, wishing I hadn't said it. How stupid did I sound?

He laughed and opened his sandwich to show me the pinkish-brown slab inside. "It's Spam."

"Spam?" I stared at it.

He put the top bread back on and took a big bite. Speaking around his mouthful, he said "You have no clue what it is, do you?"

I shook my head.

"It's canned meat. Pork."

"Canned?"

He laughed again. "Yeah. Comes in a rectangular can— hence the shape—and you pop the lid off and there it is. It's real popular here on the islands. Auntie Akamai slices it up and fries it for the sandwiches."

"Canned pork." I peeked into my sandwich. It was actually surprisingly tasty for something from a can. "I had no idea they put meat in a can. I mean, other than tuna."

"Most mainlanders think it's gross."

I squinted up at him. The sun was behind him, giving him a halo. "I kind of like it."

He smiled and I smiled back, a warm tingly feeling flowing over me.

It must be the Spam.

"Hey," he said, looking at his feet. "There's this restaurant at the resort, Sir Spamalot's. Have you seen it?" After I shook my head, he went on. "It specializes in Spam...obviously. Maybe we could, um, go for dinner sometime?"

The tingly feeling rushed over me like a wave again. *He was asking me out!*

"I mean," he went on hurriedly, "you know, to introduce you to Hawaiian cuisine at its finest. Since you'll be around for a while."

He could phrase it however he wanted. It was a *date.*

I smiled and took another bite of my sandwich. "Sure." But when I swallowed, the bite went like a rock to the pit of my stomach. I'd love to "be around," but if that detective thinks I had anything to do with Joey's death...then no more Spam for me.

CHAPTER SIX

———

When Kahiau announced we were done for the day, I thought I had never before heard such wonderful words from a more beautiful human being.

I was exhausted.

And I had to walk back to Auntie Akamai's. So off I trudged along the road, keeping the ocean in view. I should've walked along the beach, as it was probably more direct, but I knew this route and wasn't completely sure I'd recognize my shack from the ocean side. When a car pulled to the side in front of me, my heart leapt with anticipation that it was someone I might know well enough to be comfortable accepting a ride from.

Unfortunately, it was someone I had met before, and no, I wasn't comfortable accepting a ride from him.

"Want a ride?" Detective Ray leaned out his window as I came alongside the car. "I was headed to Mrs. Akamai's to talk to you anyway."

Oh *come on.*

"I'm more than happy to just follow you there if you aren't comfortable getting in my car." His brown eyes danced with silent laughter.

I hesitated by his car for a moment longer, but the exhaustion in my bones won out. As I walked around to get in, I saw Samantha the surf instructor peddling by on a bike across the street. She waved. Well, at least she'd know who picked me up, assuming she knew who Detective Ray was.

"Thank you." I climbed in.

"So, where are you from, Kiki?" The detective looked straight out the front window.

"You already know. Why are you asking?" I crossed my

arms, then quickly uncrossed them, remembering a video I had watched about body language. I didn't want to look stubborn and withholding. I just wanted to *be* stubborn and withholding.

"I'm curious what you will say." He turned his face toward me. His eyes had crinkles around them, suggesting he was older than the Hawaiian shirt made him look.

"I'm from New York," I sighed. "But it doesn't mean I knew that guy. Joey. New York is a big place."

He nodded, his attention out the front window again as he made the turn into Auntie Akamai's drive. "I've heard it is."

I opened the door as soon as the car stopped. He was slower to get out but caught up quickly with his long legs. He got to Auntie Akamai's door and was knocking before I had the chance to go around the side of the house, so I reluctantly followed him. I had been hoping to keep Auntie Akamai from hearing anything, but here she was, ushering us in.

"What can I do for you, Ray?" She led us to her small but well-appointed kitchen where she started coffee and began shuffling in a pantry for "nibbles."

"I just have a few more questions for Miss Hepburn," he said, sitting at a dinette table.

Auntie Akamai nodded, but said nothing.

I sat across from him and waited. It was a long wait. First the coffee had to be prepared and poured, then the snacks held up to my face until I accepted one, all while they had a small-talk conversation. Finally, he looked over at me.

"So, you are from New York, as is our dead man. You say the first time you met him was on the boat."

I nodded, and then we sat in silence long enough for me to squirm. "So what more can I tell you?" My mouth was very dry from the cookie, but the coffee was too strong for me. I gave it a tiny sip.

"How is it, then, that he knew you?" Detective Ray stared at me impassively.

"I have no idea." My mind started racing, perhaps from the sip of coffee. "Wait, why do you think he knew me?"

"Kahiau said he asked if he knew whether or not you were traveling alone."

Huh. So my parents think I ran off with someone?

Interesting. "Well, I never saw him before. Maybe he knew my… Maybe he was looking for a single girl to hit on."

"You said he never said or did anything inappropriate."

"He didn't…" I was interrupted by a flash of green and a flapping of wings.

"*Cracker*!" screamed Paulie.

"Yes, yes, I'll get you a cracker." Auntie Akamai hurried away to fetch a treat for her bird, who was now bobbing up and down like he was dancing and repeatedly squawking "cracker!"

The interview was effectively over, thanks to Paulie. Detective Ray gave me a hard look, then bid goodbye to Paulie and me and left me sitting and staring into the black depths of my coffee.

It sounded like Detective Ray knew Joey had sought me out. But he confused me, not just outright asking. He wanted me to offer information. Information which would make me look suspicious.

I was still pondering, staring into the blackness, when Auntie Akamai spoke. She had come back and sat across from me without me even noticing she had returned.

"I'm sorry, what?" I looked up at her.

Her kind face was creased. "I told you to spill."

"What?" I stared at her.

"I don't know what you aren't telling the police, but you had better tell me right now." She leaned back and folded her arms across her ample bosom. Paulie was on her shoulder, and I could imagine his arms folded as he stared at me too. Her eyebrows rose, and she waited. "Spill it, girlie.

"Spill?"

"The tea." Paulie made a few gulping noises, which in any other situation would have been hilarious. Auntie Akamai continued with a wave of her hand. "Give me the scoop. Whatever you young people call it these days."

"About?"

"Don't play dumb, young lady. Tell me what your deal is, or I won't be able to help you."

"Help me?" Or maybe go straight to the detective…

"You need help, right? To not get arrested for murder?" Auntie Akamai tipped her head, funnily into Paulie's little green one.

"Muuuurrrrdeeerrrr," crooned Paulie. That was super creepy.

"Oh. Right." I stared back down at my coffee and considered.

"So, spill it," Auntie Akamai said impatiently and was promptly echoed by Paulie.

"Okay. So, it looks like this Joey guy was sent by my parents to take me home. He made it sound like he'd been following me for a few weeks to find me. He said I had to go with him or else." I spoke to the coffee cup, afraid of her reaction.

"Why?"

"Why what?" I gave a quick glance up, and she gave me a squinty eyeball. "Okay. I left to travel. I wanted to go diving."

I glanced up, and she just stared at me through slitted eyes.

"My parents are very…wealthy. My mother expects me to marry rich and is constantly going on about eligible men, and looking the part, and so on." I couldn't seem to stop now that I started. "She isn't supportive of me doing my own thing or being myself. She wants me to be a little version of her. Doesn't want me working unless it's somewhere where I might meet a rich guy."

When I stopped to take a breath, Auntie Akamai broke in.

"And your father?"

"He wants me to work at his company. Well, his father's company, and I'm expected to be the next Barrington in charge. But I have no interest in it. He was fine with me studying whatever I wanted in school, with the assumption I would work in his company in the end." To my embarrassment, my eyes stung. I could see his crestfallen face in my mind. I turned my face toward the window.

"What is his company?"

"Um. He's a businessman. He works in real estate." Wasn't exactly a lie.

"Like an agent?" If she noticed my moist eyes, she didn't act like she did.

"No, like a developer. He builds…um…hotels, resorts, conference centers. Like Aloha Lagoon." I watched the palm fronds tremble in the breeze.

"Did he make Aloha Lagoon?"

"*Aloha*!" Paulie squawked.

I looked at Paulie and hoped her question would be forgotten with the bird's outburst. But when I looked back at her, no dice. She was looking into my face with raised eyebrows.

"No," I sighed. "But a similar one on Maui."

Auntie Akamai nodded. "Okay." She sat and watched me for a minute before going on. "So you ran away from home. At…how old are you?"

"Twenty-two. And I didn't 'run away.' I'm…traveling."

Auntie Akamai shook her head, chuckling. "I was married and had two kids by your age." Then she sobered. "You ran away from home—pardon me, went *traveling*—at twenty-two on your parents' dime because they wanted you to get married or work. You ran away, which is a childish thing to do, because they wanted you to grow up."

I sat up straight. "I didn't run away," I spit out. "I just want to dive. Travel. See the world before I have to go and be boring." I crossed my arms and hunched back into the chair. "I have a deadline."

Auntie Akamai studied me. "Deadline?"

I stubbornly looked away again.

"So did you kill that man to keep him from taking you home?"

"No! Of course not! I was willing to go. I didn't want to, but I'd go. My bag was all packed and everything. You can ask Dex—he saw it." I thought back to when he helped me move. He hadn't said anything about the already-packed suitcase, but he had to have seen it. I think.

"When is the last time you've spoken with your parents?"

I fiddled with the mug handle before glancing up sheepishly. "Two months."

"You've been traveling who knows where, doing who knows what, and diving, which can be dangerous. Can you even imagine how worried they must be?! If my kids didn't call for two days, I'd be hectic!" Auntie Akamai's eyes flashed.

Paulie clicked his beak and swayed back and forth. Auntie Akamai reached a hand up to stroke his feathers. "Now, now, baby bird. I'm not mad at you."

"My parents are not like you. I doubt they were worried. My mother isn't exactly…mothery." I threw my hands up. "She comes from old money. My father grew up watching his father build the company from the ground up. But he tends to agree with her to keep Mrs. Barrington happy."

Paulie screeched and then said "Barrington." He spread out the consonants, and I almost smiled.

"That's what you call your mother?"

"Not to her face. No, she's 'Mother.'" I said it in the snootiest voice I could manage.

"Okay." She waved a hand. "So what is it you want to do besides travel and dive?"

I pursed my lips. "I want to work in Marine Biology. I want to work somewhere like Aloha Lagoon Diving. I want to spend my day with fish and nights with people who actually care about me." I looked out the window again. "I'd like a boyfriend that isn't handpicked by my mother. I'd like to live somewhere pretty and watch the sunrise. I'd like to take care of myself and make decisions without dreading what my mother will say." I paused and took a breath. "I got a taste of being my own person during college, and now the thought of going back to that life is…I just can't."

When I turned back to her, Auntie Akamai was watching me with her hands folded on the table.

"And now you are taking care of yourself and making your own decisions and are the only person with a connection to this murdered man."

I'm not much of a crier, but when she said that, everything caught up to me. A tear escaped and ran down my cheek.

Paulie was watching me with those beady eyes. He clicked his beak and crooned, "Now, now baby bird, now now."

CHAPTER SEVEN

———

It probably wasn't due to the tear, but Auntie Akamai agreed to help me figure things out.

Well, after making me say multiple times *I did not kill Joey* while staring into her eyes while she held my wrist, checking my pulse. Apparently she was a walking, talking lie-detector machine.

Sufficiently convinced, she pulled a laptop out of a drawer and plunked it in front of me. "Can't stand the thing, but I'm sure you know how to use it."

I started it up then waited ten minutes for her to search for the password (it was *Paulie*), and then I checked for local news. There was nothing about the dead man.

"Well, we can't very well Google 'Joey' and expect something to pop up." I snapped the laptop shut and leaned back. "We don't even know his last name. I wish I had thought to look for him in the logbook when I had a chance."

Auntie Akamai leaned against her kitchen counter and tapped her lip with her index finger. "Hmmm. I have a friend who works at the resort." She abruptly walked out of the kitchen. *Okay.*

I heard her talking in the other room, so I opened the laptop again and poked in the password. Paulie glared at me from the back of the opposite chair. "I'm sure it's fine," I said to him. "I'm going to check my email."

I navigated to the web-based option for my email and clicked open the inbox. I had over a hundred unread emails, but most were from stores or websites I had shopped on in the past. I selected those and sent them to the junk mail folder in hopes that the email system would send them straight there next time. The remaining dozen or so were from my parents, friends from college, and a neighbor. All were asking when I was coming back, what happened, why was I gone...except the lone one from my mother, which simply said *Cutting off your funds*.

Thanks, Mother. Nice chat. My cursor hovered over the message, wanting to send it to the junk folder too. I resisted.

At least the ones from my father were a little more concerned-sounding. *Just let us know you're okay*. And *your mother is so upset*. I rolled my eyes and started to close the web browser, then had second thoughts. I opened the email that entreated me to "just let them know" and typed in a quick note. *I'm fine*, I told him. *Found a job. Enjoying myself*. I signed it with the pet name he had for me, and after taking a deep breath, I closed my eyes and hit Send.

I had heard Auntie Akamai speaking louder, but it didn't really register, so when a voice spoke while my eyes were closed, I almost jumped out of my Gucci slides.

"Whoa, sorry," said Dex, holding his hands out in front of him. "I didn't mean to startle you."

"It's fine," I said and quickly shut down the web browser and closed the computer.

He smiled at me then, but Paulie had some choice words for him. He squawked several curse words at Dex, calling him, shall I say, "a donkey's behind," and several other sailor-worthy words.

I gasped. "My, my Paulie, you kiss Auntie Akamai with that beak?!"

"That's what I get for teaching him swear words," Dex said, his face red. He slid onto the remaining chair—the one without the foul-mouthed parrot.

"Dex! Are you teaching him more bad words!?" Auntie Akamai yelled from the other room.

"No, Auntie. He was just reminding us I had." Dex looked at me, still mortified. He didn't smile again until I started giggling.

Auntie Akamai walked in and smacked him on the side of his head, which made me laugh more. But she had a smile too.

"You're still my favorite *keiki*," she said, patting him on the shoulder. "Even though you've poisoned my baby's tongue."

"What is *keiki*?" I asked.

"Nephew," she said, tousling his hair and making him blush again. "Did you not know Kahiau is my brother?"

"No," I gaped. "I thought they called you Auntie like a term of endearment. I didn't know it was literal."

"It is." She smiled broadly. "But you can still call me Auntie." She turned to Dex. "What brings you by?"

"I was, um, checking to make sure Kiki got home okay." He looked at me. "Looks like you did."

"Yes, I did."

Auntie Akamai remained silent, thankfully, about the policeman driving me home.

"Okay." Dex looked around and fidgeted. "That's good."

I nodded. "It's not far."

"No, not really."

Auntie Akamai watched us flounder without throwing either of us a lifeline.

Dex looked back and forth between us. "Well, okay then. I'll…be going now."

Auntie Akamai turned to me after he left with raised eyebrows and a knowing smirk.

I felt the heat rising in my cheeks. "What?"

She just chuckled and waved me toward the kitchen. "Come, I'll make us some dinner."

* * *

I didn't sleep as well that night, restless with dreams of bodies under the water and snake tattoos. Exhausted and not feeling particularly well (probably from eating the canned pork stuff twice, as Auntie Akamai had made eggs and Spam for dinner), I headed out to work. I waved to Auntie Akamai as I passed her window.

It didn't take long to get to the dive shop on foot, maybe ten minutes along the beach. (I wasn't going to risk seeing the detective again.) I felt better by the time I got there, the fresh air clearing out my head, my toes in the sand and water. But when I popped into the shop, Kahiau and Dex were having a heated discussion, which stopped abruptly when they saw me. Dex gave his father a long glare, then brushed past me without a word, slamming the door behind him.

Confused, I stared at the door.

"Um, Kiki, I need to have a word with you."

My heart fell under the soles of my bare feet. *Oh no.*

Kahiau spoke again, right behind me. "Kiki..."

I turned slowly and gazed up at him. "Yes?"

"We...uh, well, I..." He frowned at his shoes. "I'm going to need you to stay home until this murder stuff is worked out."

Did I just get fired?

"You still have your job. We...I just don't want the clients spooked by any rumors. You understand?" He looked at me with concerned eyes.

"Okay," I whispered.

"Here," he said, hurrying over to a bookshelf that held some fish identification books. "You can use the time to study up. I'll still pay you for part time. Does that sound okay?" He returned with a stack, which he held out to me.

"Thank you," I whispered. I took the books and fled.

I didn't make it far before Dex caught me.

"Kiki, stop," he called. "Wait a second."

"Why?" I stopped and turned on him.

"I...are you okay?" He spread his hands in front of him.

"Um, no, I'm not. I got fired my second day on the job." I scowled at him. "You could've given me a heads up. Like last night? Is that why you came to the house?"

"No. I saw you get into the detective's car. I was thinking you would tell me why." He turned and gestured at the sea helplessly. "But you said nothing."

I blew out a breath and fought back the tears that were threatening my eyes. "Because it is nothing." I squeezed the books tighter to my chest. "I did nothing. That was the first time I met that guy Joey."

He stared at me a long moment.

"Do you not believe me?" I glared back at him.

He turned and looked toward the sea.

"You...you think I killed him?" My arms went slack, and the books fell to the sand.

"Well, we don't exactly know you, Kiki. You've told me—us—nothing about yourself." He squatted and started picking up the books. "You're secretive."

I turned around, but he stood and grabbed my arm.

"Let go of me," I growled.

He was trying to turn me toward him, pulling me to him, leaning into me. Before I realized what I was doing, I had my arms around him too…

Then I came to my senses, put my hands against his chest, and shoved. He stumbled back, while I turned and sprinted down the beach.

*   *   *

A shadow fell across my face, causing me to open my eyes and squint up to see who it was.

"You okay, girlie?" Auntie Akamai blocked out the sun I had been enjoying. Well, the sun I was trying to enjoy.

"Yeah." I sighed and sat up, shading my face to look at her. I had made it as far as the beach behind her house and thought I'd relax awhile since I was a lady of leisure again. "I guess you know?"

"Yes. But no time to mope about." She gestured for me to get up. "Let's go!"

"Where?" I said, standing and brushing off the sand from my shorts.

"The resort. My friend on the staff is going to sneak us into the dead guy's room."

I couldn't help but gasp. "Auntie Akamai!"

She waved a hand. "Shush. We'll just take a little peek. At least find out the man's last name so you can properly goggle him."

"Google," I corrected, and despite my feeling of apprehension, followed her to her car. "And his name is Joey. We probably shouldn't call him 'dead guy.'"

She tossed a set of keys to me as we approached her car, but being completely unprepared to catch something (and not too good at it anyway), they simply bounced off me and landed on the ground. I bent to pick them up and handed them back to her.

She stared at me. "I was asking you to drive."

"Oh...I don't drive."

"Don't, won't, or can't?" Auntie Akamai's dark eyes bored into my own.

"I never learned how. Never needed to in the city." I shrugged. "It's not a big deal. It's pretty common, really."

She nodded slowly, then went to the driver's side, lowering herself into the seat with a groan. "You should learn. It's part of being independent."

I sat on the passenger's side but didn't reply. On the short ride to the resort, she filled me in on the plan she and her friend had come up with.

Driving brazenly into the staff lot, Auntie Akamai parked like she belonged there. After heaving herself out of the car, she walked toward a back door. Once we got to the door, she gave a series of knocks ("The secret code.") and waited. She turned to me abruptly and handed me a hair tie.

"Bind up that hair." She nodded at my loose locks. "Can't risk leaving any behind."

She sounded like a pro at breaking and entering.

A short Polynesian man opened the door. He leaned out to look left and right and then waved us in. We entered what appeared to be a handyman shop, tools hanging on the walls and a long, tall table littered with all kinds of interesting things. I went over for a closer look but clasped my hands behind my back. I didn't want to get yelled at for touching things.

"Kiki, this is Ikaika... Ikaika, this is Kiki." Auntie Akamai flip-flopped a hand between us. "I told her the plan in the car."

He nodded. "Good. Let's go, then."

CHAPTER EIGHT

———

Ikaika left his shop through a door on the opposite side from where we'd come in. He carried a work bag with him. We counted to ten then slipped out into a hall in the hotel. We followed him at a distance, trailing him to the second floor. He stopped and knocked on a door, waited a moment, and then unlocked it, propping it open. As we continued, we passed the one with a "no entry—police evidence" sticker. That must have been Joey's room.

We slid into the room where Ikaika was waiting by the connecting door. He unlocked it, ushered us in, then closed it quietly behind us. He would stand watch as well as keep in contact with a coworker in the lobby.

Once in the room, we stood and looked around. It wasn't the cleanest, clutter-wise. Auntie Akamai fished into a pocket of her voluminous muumuu to pull out two pair of latex gloves. I raised my eyebrows at her but slipped them on. It certainly wouldn't do to be caught having been here.

Auntie Akamai began to methodically go through the drawers, leaving me to wonder if she had done this before. She certainly had been prepared for it!

I was poking around in the bathroom (Brut aftershave and a cheap disposable razor did nothing to redeem Joey in my mind) when Auntie Akamai called to me.

"Check this out," she said in a loud whisper, pointing to something on the desk. I hurried over and took a look.

Joseph Morton, Private Investigator said a cheaply printed business card, followed by contact information and adorned with a cheesy but artistic eyeball. I fished my phone out of my pocket and took a picture.

A blank notepad sat there on the desk as well, prompting

Auntie Akamai to procure a pencil from somewhere and lightly rub it over the top sheet.

"Ah-ha!" she whispered. She pointed.

Katherine Barrington = "Kiki Hepburn" Room 258

I stared at it. "Do you think the police took the top sheet?"

She shrugged. "I'd think they'd take the whole thing. But I don't know." She carefully pulled the sheet she'd dirtied off the pad, folded it, and went to tuck it in into a pocket but dropped it. It fluttered under the desk.

"I'll get it." I got down on my hands and knees and reached under the desk. That's when I noticed a piece of paper tucked into the label stapled to the bottom of the desk. Curious, I tugged it out and sat up, whacking my head on the desk.

Auntie Akamai peered down at me. "What are you doing under there? Are you trying to break the desk?"

Rubbing my head, I stood and held out the two pieces of paper. Her folded one made it into the pocket this time, while she smoothed out the other one on the surface of the desk.

The paper was from a notepad helpfully labeled *From the desk of Joseph Morton, PI.* It was a list of some kind, with letters and numbers in lines. It made no sense. Auntie Akamai and I leaned into each other to look at it.

"Let's take a picture. We can study it later."

I did as she suggested, then refolded it. "We could just take it. They didn't find it before. Or do I put it back where I found it?"

I heard a vibration coming from deep within Auntie Akamai's dress. She fished out her phone and looked at it. "Uh-oh, time to go," she whispered. She gestured at the desk. "Put it back. Wouldn't do to be caught with his notepaper, now would it?"

I dropped to the floor and hurriedly shoved it back into its hiding place.

We hurried to the connecting door, stripping off our gloves. Auntie Akamai deposited them in a pocket.

Ikaika was waiting. "The police are in the lobby," he said. "Let's hurry."

I took one last look at the room as Ikaika was closing the

door.

The note had fallen and was now on the floor.

"Wait!" I pointed, but Auntie Akamai tugged on my arm.

"It's too late," she hissed. "Don't worry about it." Ikaika poked his head out the door, then waved us on. "Coast clear. Let's go."

We hurried back down the back stairwells and to his door labeled *Maintenance Only*.

"Find anything interesting?" he asked after the door was safely closed behind us.

Auntie Akamai told him about the business card and the notes.

"A private investigator, huh?" He rubbed his stubbly chin. "Makes sense, I suppose."

I nodded. "It does. And it opens up a whole lot of motives from other people. Now we have to figure out who knew him and why they hated him enough to kill him."

Ikaika and Auntie Akamai both nodded. "Good luck," added Ikaika.

He opened the exterior door, looking around before opening it wider for us to go through.

"Thank you, Mr. Ikaika." I smiled at him.

He laughed. "Just Ikaika is fine, and you're welcome."

We got into the car, and Auntie Akamai backed out of the space and turned toward the exit.

And almost ran over Detective Ray.

"Oh fudge," whispered Auntie Akamai.

My mind echoed what she said but made the word a little spicier.

Detective Ray squinted into the car, then waved us to stop as we rolled past.

Sighing, Auntie Akamai put the car in park and rolled down the window. "Detective Ray, how are you?"

"Fine, fine. And what brings you here today?" He leaned down and looked at the two of us.

"I brought Kiki here to meet about getting a job," Auntie Akamai lied smoothly.

"Really?" Detective Ray directed at me. "Which department?"

"Housekeeping," said Auntie Akamai at the same time I said, "Spa."

There was a terrifyingly long pause before Auntie Akamai chuckled. "Yep, keeping options open. Just inquiring about where they might have an opening."

"What happened to working at the dive shop?" He tipped his head, watching me.

I shrugged. "They wanted me to take a break."

"Sorry to hear that," he said. "Did they tell you about the dive weights?" Detective Ray was looking directly into my face, I think. He had sunglasses on, so I couldn't be sure.

I shook my head.

"The ones strapped on the victim were from Aloha Lagoon Diving. Some of the stolen ones."

My heart froze. At my side, Auntie Akamai stiffened.

"Easily a coincidence, Ray," she said.

"Sure. But is it a coincidence that Kiki's room here at the resort"—he gestured behind him—"was paid for by the same credit card which paid for the victim's? Or that you and he arrived the same day?"

Auntie Akamai didn't say anything.

"Would you step out of the car so we can speak more privately?"

"Sure." I moved to get out and somehow managed to. It felt like my limbs were numb, and I was worried they wouldn't work. I caught Auntie Akamai's eye as I closed the door. She looked worried.

I met Detective Ray in front of the car.

"So is there anything you want to tell me?" He folded his arms across his chest and tipped his head.

I tried to shake my head, but it wouldn't move for me. I realized with embarrassment I was shaking, probably visibly.

"Miss Barrington?" he prompted. *Not Kiki Hepburn.*

"He was sent by my parents to bring me home," I whispered.

Detective Ray leaned forward to hear me better.

"He told me when we got out of the van after the dive." I raised a shaking hand to my hair, realized it was still bound up, and pulled the hair tie out. I ran my fingers through it to try to relax.

"And what did you say?"

"Nothing. He said to meet him at ten on the patio the next morning, but he never showed up." I lifted a hand imploringly. "You have to believe me. I didn't have anything to do with him being drowned."

"He wasn't drowned." Detective Ray frowned right after he said it. *He didn't mean to tell me that.* He cleared his throat. "So would you not want to go with him?"

I shook my head. "He was creepy, so of course not."

Detective Ray looked perplexed. "I mean, did you not want to go home?"

"No, not really, but I knew I'd have to go home at some point." I felt the heat rising in my cheeks. "When I turn twenty-three, my allowance is cut off. So the fantasy of jetting around the world diving would come to an end in a few months anyway."

"Allowance," repeated the detective. He gave a short shake of his head, then straightened to his full height. "Are you aware of anyone else here knowing the victim?"

I shook my head.

"And where were you the night of the dive? The first dive."

My eyes widened slightly. "Was that when he was killed?"

The detective pursed his lips, clearly annoyed. "I know you didn't check out of the resort for another two days. So what did you do that night?"

I looked at the ground, my fingers separating a section of hair to twirl around my finger—my nervous habit. *Would it be better to look nervous or not look nervous?*

"Miss Barrington," Detective Ray prompted.

"Oh, right. I was at the Lava Pot with some other people. Casey, the bartender…I don't know his last name…he'll verify. I sat with Samantha…I don't know her last name either." I frowned. *Why don't I remember last names?*

"I know who they are. I also know you left around eleven thirty with Dex Kekoa." He crossed her arms and stared down at me.

"He simply walked me to my room," I said defensively.

"At eleven thirty?"

"I guess so, yes. I don't know what time it was!" I almost rolled my eyes but managed to stop myself.

"Okay. I'm going to need you to come to the station to give a DNA sample."

"DNA?" I echoed. "Like blood?"

"No, hair." He gestured at the locks I was rolling around my finger.

There was a knocking on the window of the car. "Detective Ray," Auntie Akamai called out the window.

We turned to look at her, but she was gesturing past us. We both turned to look at a small woman, propped on a car hood with a camera. She was at a good distance away, but when she saw that we'd spotted her, she popped up and hurried away, sliding between two bushes.

"What? Who was that?" I looked back at Detective Ray.

He sighed. "She's our local nosey reporter. Steer clear of her please." He glowered at me. "And come to the station in the morning." He raised a hand in farewell to Auntie Akamai, gave me one last long look, and walked away.

I went and got into the car. "Who was that woman?"

"Felicity Chase. She's a pain in the patootie."

"A reporter?"

Auntie Akamai nodded. "Believes herself to be an investigative reporter but in reality writes tabloid-level trash." She grunted. "I don't believe she's allowed to be on resort property, which is probably why she hightailed it."

She recited a list of the articles the reporter had written, sounding a bit more like a fan girl than a disgusted reader. But regardless, I was to steer clear, which was no problem. I wasn't a complete enigma to the paparazzi at home, but it wasn't a daily problem by any means.

I sure hoped it wasn't going to be here.

CHAPTER NINE

―――

After my crapola day, I decided I needed a stiff drink. I headed for The Lava Pot, and as soon as I walked in, Casey saw me and started mixing up a mai tai for me. Samantha was there too, so I hopped onto a stool next to hers.

"Looks like you've had a rough day," she observed, giving me a once over.

"You could say that." I ran a hand through my hair, instantly reminding myself of Detective Ray's request. "Kahiau insisted I wasn't fired, but he told me to not go back to work until this murder stuff is cleared up."

"How is the investigation going?" She leaned toward me with her voice lowered. "I mean, are you investigating?"

The hair on the back of my neck stood on end. Had someone seen me in the hotel? "Why would I?"

Samantha blushed. "Just wondering."

What did she know?

But before I could ask, I was pulled into a chokehold-slash-hug from behind.

"Oooo, I've missed you soooo much!" Ainsley slurred into my hair. "Little Katherine Bore-ington." She hiccupped and released me, sliding in sideways onto the stool on my side opposite of Samantha.

"Boreington?" Samantha looked at me, horrified.

I patted Ainsley's cheek. "Yes, that was my nickname from the more…adventurous girls."

Ainsley giggled but had the decency to blush. "You knew?"

I raised my eyebrows. "Hard not to." I turned to Samantha. "Someone wrote my number on the bathroom wall at school with the message *For a dull time, call Katherine*

Boreington."

Samantha frowned. "That was mean."

I shrugged. "It was an all-girl school. And you know how girls are."

I turned back to Ainsley. "Where's your fiancé?" I turned back to Samantha and stage-whispered, "She's marrying her best friend's father. He's also her ex-boyfriend's father." *Ainsley wasn't the only one who could be catty!*

Samantha's mouth fell open, and she peered around me at Ainsley.

Ainsley laughed. "He's richer than some small nations, so oh well! And he is soooo good in—ow!" Her head jerked back suddenly, and her hands flew up, spilling her drink on me.

Claire stood behind her, seething, a hank of Ainsley's hair in her hand. "Don't worry. Daddy can pay for new extensions!"

Ainsley swung around and launched herself at Claire. "So you're going to steal mine! So like you." She grabbed Claire's hair in retaliation, and with a grunt they fell to the floor in a pile of designer clothes and shrieks.

The fight got Casey's attention, and he hurried around the bar. I pulled halfheartedly at Ainsley while he helped Claire up.

"Ladies, let's cool down or you'll have to leave." Casey glared at the two of them. "You understand?"

The two of them glowered at each other until they actually looked at Casey.

Ainsley put out a hand to Casey's chest and purred, "Maybe you should spank us."

Claire giggled too, bringing her face as close to Casey's as she could get, which, due to the difference in height, wasn't all that close. "Me first."

Casey's eyebrows rose, and he cleared his throat and glanced at me before addressing the troublemakers again. "All right, ladies, let's behave or I will call security." He gave them one last stern look before dropping his grip and turning away. He weaved through the gathered crowd, shaking his head.

Claire's and Ainsley's statements got the attention of a gaggle of college-aged men though, and they were immediately invited back to a table for drinks. Claire went, but Ainsley made a big deal of waving her diamond around.

"I'm *engaged*, you scoundrel!" she crowed. She turned back to the bar, muttering, "like you make any money." Draping her arm around my shoulder, she pulled me too close for comfort, her cocktail-laced breath in my face. "So sorry about your top," she said, wiping my drink-soaked T-shirt with a cocktail napkin. "At least it's cheap."

I frowned and pushed her away. "It's fine. I'm sorry about your hair."

Her hand flew to the back of her head. "Does it look bad?"

I nodded. "Terrible." I hadn't even seen it yet, but she deserved it.

She felt the back of her head for a moment, then shrugged. "So," she said, pulling me into her side again. "Tell me about this murder thing."

"How did you know about that?" I asked.

"Oh, sweetheart, everyone is talking about it. And that you are suspect number one."

My stomach clenched. *Was she just getting even with me?* I glanced at Samantha, who was frowning, then back to Ainsley. Her face was two inches from mine, and I could tell she'd had shrimp for dinner. "What are you talking about?"

"Oh sweetie. I saw the cheaply dressed policeman talking to you. What happened? Did the hairy man get too friendly with you?" She shook her head. "I can imagine. I mean, you are fairly attractive, and he was disgusting." She drew out the last word. "Ugh, he needed a serious wax job."

How did she know that?

I leaned back so I could see her whole face. "Did you know him?"

"No, no, of course not." She dropped her arm and turned to the bar. "I heard about him from…Claire."

Well, that could be believable if she had said it more convincingly. And hadn't just been rolling on the floor fighting her. "You didn't know him?"

"No, no, no, of course not." She waved her hand around. "How would *I* know *him*?"

The lady doth protest too much, methinks.

I leaned in conspiratorially. "Did you know he was a private investigator from the city?"

She arranged her face into *shock*. "No! From New York?"

I nodded. "Yes. I wonder who he was here investigating?" I glanced around to see if anyone else could hear me. Samantha was looking the other way, watching Casey at the other end of the bar.

Ainsley's eyes narrowed. "I heard he was here for you."

My blood froze in my veins. "What makes you think that?"

She snickered. "Heather." She primped at her hair, then continued. "I guess he questioned her or something after your little diving trip."

Except he already knew who I was before the dive trip. Right? Why else would he have gone on it?

She was watching me with such clear, conniving eyes I had to wonder if the drunk behavior was an act. She leaned in and put a hand on my arm. "Was he after you? Did he say something to you?"

I studied her. I trusted her about as far as I could throw her. And she was definitely heavier than me.

Oh, wait a sec.

"How did Heather know who he was?" I watched her closely.

She stared at me. "I…I don't know. She must've heard it from resort staff. Or maybe the police?"

Aha. "But I just now told you he was a private investigator, and you were shocked. Then you said Heather told you he was here investigating me. Which is it?"

"Oh, there you are, Sugar Buns," Ned said from behind us.

You've got to be kidding. Perfect timing. I turned to look at Ainsley's fiancé-slash-Claire's dad. He had to be at least midforties, but other than his "dad bod" tummy pooch, he was well built. His sandy brown hair was the same color as his son Todd's, but thankfully he didn't wear it in a mullet too. His eyes did crinkle attractively when he smiled at Ainsley, but I'm not sure that would have been enough to woo me.

"Oh, Papa Bear, I'm so happy to see you!" Ainsley squealed.

I bet you are.

They wrapped their arms around each other and started making out. I looked away and saw Samantha watching with a stricken look on her face. She made eye contact with me, and I fake vomited. She nodded.

They came up for air, whispered things I want to bleach from my brain, then darted away, hand in hand. I watched them leave, sad I didn't get a clear answer but also relieved they took their PDA somewhere else. Hopefully somewhere less *P*.

"Aren't they absolutely disgusting?"

I turned to see Claire taking Ainsley's vacated stool. She shook her head. "Can you believe she's going to be my stepmother?"

I couldn't help but snort. I felt sorry for her. Well, a teeny bit. Not much. But you had to admit that was funny.

"Do you live with your mom?" I asked after putting a cocktail napkin to my nose to play off my snort as a nasal issue of some kind.

She shook her head. "Same building as all of the rest of them though." She gestured at the bartender (not Casey) and ordered a Cosmo. "You know how hard it is to find a nice place in the city."

"That must be weird."

"It is." She tossed her head. "But whatever."

"Are you upset about it? About them?" My curiosity overrode politeness at this moment, though I still cringed at my own words.

Unbelievably, she shrugged, swaying a little as she did so. "I was at first, you know. But then I figured, she always was a little loose." She nodded to the bartender as he set her drink in front of her, then pulled out the little umbrella holding maraschino cherries and ate them, continuing to speak around them. "Now I guess I feel like they are welcome to each other. They deserve each other and everything that will happen to them."

"And your mom? How's she doing?" I played with my

own little umbrella absently, more pondering her last answer than thinking about what to ask next.

She raised her shoulders again. "He was caught cheating, so the prenup was annulled. She's taken him to the cleaners!" She laughed. "Hmm." She tipped her head to the side and tapped her chin. "If only I could get Ainsley to mess around and void their prenup." She barked out a short laugh. "Then she wouldn't get squat when he inevitably trades her in for the high-schooler next door." Her face fell. "I did try to talk Todd into it, but he was being a lame-o."

Hum. "What kind of proof did they have to void the agreement?"

She stared morosely into her drink. "Pictures."

Ew. "How did they get pictures, or do I want to know?"

She looked at me, her eyes almost crossing. "That guy, the private eye." She stared into her drink again. "I tried to get him to follow her to catch her with Todd, but I never heard back. I guess he went *swimming* before that." She laughed, hiccupped, then sighed.

I frowned. "How did you know he was a PI?"

She snorted. "Heather hired him to catch 'Sugar Bear' in action."

I almost fell off my chair. I had to act nonchalant. "So why do you call your mom Heather?"

"She wants me to. Always has. Probably doesn't want anyone to think she's actually my mother." Her eyes suddenly filled with tears, and she blinked rapidly.

"So people would think you're sisters. That's kind of funny." Clearly that wasn't what she thought, but no reason to poke someone when they're already down.

She gave me the smallest of smiles. "Yeah, totally."

Casey appeared in front of us. "Miss D'Angelo, I'm cutting you off, okay? I saw those guys giving you tequila shooters over there. Would you like one of the staff to escort you safely to your room?"

Reacting slowly, she looked at him. "Will it be you?"

He smiled and said no.

"I can take you," I offered.

She looked beyond me—I thought she was just having

trouble focusing—but she smiled. "No offense," she slurred, "but I'd rather have him take me."

I turned to see who she was talking about. It was Dex, on the other side of Samantha. Our eyes met, and he quickly looked away.

"Hey!" Claire stood and stumbled away. "Sexy dive dude. Will you walk me to my room?"

Dex looked startled but took her by the arm and led her away. He didn't even take a look back at me. The only thing that made me feel better was that he was holding her elbow like he was walking a granny across the street.

CHAPTER TEN

———

At closing time, Samantha offered me a ride home, which I accepted. Walking back to Auntie Akamai's in the dark wasn't a good idea with a murderer on the loose. And all those feral chickens, too. Shudder.

When I got back to my room, I climbed into my little cot of a bed, ready for the emptiness of sleep. But it was not to be. There were too many things swirling around in my brain.

Heather had hired Joey to find evidence of Ned's cheating. Claire knew this. Did Ned?

And though she denied knowing who he was, Ainsley clearly was aware of him. Did she know what role he had played?

Did they know he was in Aloha Lagoon *before* he died?

Figuring I wasn't going to get any sleep anyway, I pulled out my phone. I found a notepad in the pantry and a pen in my purse and copied down the lines of code we'd found in Joey's room.

> *ND-TE1/2M,0/125K,0*
> *CD-CC10K,com/S&T75K,0*
> *TD-DD,R,R?25K(10K)*
> *HD-CC50K,com*
> *SJ-F500K/125K,com*
> *AR-D10K,com*

I tried separating them into sections, then just letters, then just numbers. It didn't make sense. I stared at them until my eyes started crossing, so I crawled back into my bed. I fell asleep quickly but dreamed of my prep school algebra teacher. *Determine the common denominator*, she kept telling me as I stood paralyzed in front of the white board covered top to bottom in symbols. *Look at it*, she yelled, pointing at the board. *You can figure it out. Try harder!*

The meaning of that dream was obvious.

When I woke, the sun was overhead. I sat up, rubbing my eyes and tasting my morning breath. I was startled to see a tray on the small table. A coffee carafe and a mound of food.

Padding over, I saw a note next to it.

Kiki,
You looked tired. I didn't want to wake you.
Here is your breakfast when you wake up.
I put milk & juice in the fridge.
-AA

Nice! I was starving. I dropped the note and got the milk before sitting and pouring some coffee. I started with a pastry with orange-pink fruit goo oozing out the sides.

Then it hit me. I froze, pastry halfway to my mouth. A blob of fruit goo plopped on my leg. I slowly returned the pastry to its plate and slid the note over to look at it again.

AA, for Auntie Akamai. Initials. Oh wow. *Initials?*

I hurried over to the bed and pulled the notepad from under my pillow. I stared at the sheath of papers.

The first section of the lines were all two letters, and obviously had similar meanings since they were arranged the same way. I smacked my forehead with my hand.

ND, Ned D'Angelo. *CD*, Claire. *TD*, Todd. *HD*, Heather. It took me a moment, but then I figured *AR* was Ainsley Rickenbacker!

I started laughing and slumped back into the chair, shaking with my mirth. Then it occurred to me.

"The dead man wrote all their initials…this proves they all knew him." I stared at the sheet. *Wow.*

The only initials I couldn't figure out were SJ. If you look at the group, who else would be included in this grouping of names? So I only had that and the rest of the lines to figure out.

No problem.

I propped the notepad up to stare at as I ate, but there were no more lightning strikes.

After I was full, I went out to the beach. I sat with my toes in the sand and watched the waves come in. I started writing the codes in the sand, having them pretty much committed to memory by now. I had just finished Claire's line when a wave swept up and washed the second half of it away, everything after the *com*. I stared at it. Was that supposed to be dot-com, like a website? But not all of them had the com, and the punctuation that preceded it looked more like a comma than a period.

"I'll have to look those up on the internet and see," I muttered as I watched the wave wash the rest of the code away. I started doodling a stick figure fleeing the waves as his buddy succumbed to them.

I headed inside and showered, leaving my hair loose for my DNA sample-giving. Going around the side of the house, I stood and looked at the bike leaning against the wall.

"*Lady*!"

I jumped out of my skin. Paulie was inside the window above the bicycle, watching me.

"*Lady want a cracker*!" he screeched.

"Hi Paulie."

"*Pretty lady! Pretty bird!*"

"Aww, thanks." I smiled at the parrot. I felt much more comfortable with his presence when there was a barrier between us. "You're much sweeter than those wild chickens, aren't you?"

"*Chicken*," he repeated.

"Are you calling my parrot a chicken?" Auntie Akamai said at my elbow.

I jumped at the sound of her voice and patted my chest as I turned to her. "You startled me."

She gave a small smile. "I can see that." She leaned toward the window. "Hello, sweetums."

Paulie made kissing sounds and whistled.

Auntie Akamai turned back to me. "Where are you off to?"

I looked at the bike. "The police station. I need to give my hair sample."

Auntie Akamai grunted. "Except you don't remember how to ride a bike, do you?" She laughed. "There's a reason the saying says, 'it's like riding a bike.' You'll be fine."

"Except I've never ridden a bike," I mumbled. I could see her head move in my periphery, but I was too embarrassed to look at her.

"Hmm. Maybe Dex can teach you."

Now I did look at her. "No," I said a little too firmly. "I'll just walk."

Her eyebrows rose, but she let it slide by.

I turned to leave, then remembered. "Thank you for breakfast, by the way. Your note actually helped me make headway with those codes from Joey's room."

"Oh?" Her head tipped. "Want to share?"

"You signed your note *AA*, which made me realize the first two letters of each code were initials." I pulled out my phone and showed her, reading off the names. Except, of course, the one I didn't know.

"Who are those people?"

I sighed. "I know them from New York."

"Your…social circle?" She looked down, smoothing her muumuu.

"Sort of. I went to school with the girls." I pointed at the initials of my former classmates.

"So I guess they all knew the dead man too, if he had their initials. That's good, for you." She tapped her lip. "We just need to figure out the rest of the code." She squinted down at my phone screen. "Your initials aren't there."

I looked at the screen again. "Unless the *K* is referring to me."

"Oh, I figured it was the abbreviation for thousand."

I gaped at her. Together, we bent over the tiny diagram. "Like those are dollar amounts?"

She ran her finger along Todd's line. "'Twenty-five thousand' then 'ten thousand' in the parentheses."

"Wow. Maybe so." I bit my lip, staring at the algebraic-like codes.

"Are you going to mention this to Detective Ray?"

"I don't know how I can without it coming out that we went into Joey's room." I pursed my lips.

"You could mention that there are other New Yorkers here. Let him go from there."

I shrugged. "I'm not sure why he'd find that relevant. He didn't pay for their hotel rooms."

She stared at me. "He was paying for your hotel room?"

I looked at the floor and kicked some kind of nut with my toe. "Not at first. But once my debit card was turned off, so I couldn't have a choice about leaving."

She sighed and nodded. "Well, we'll think of something." She turned to Paulie again. "Won't we, Paulie?"

* * *

Even though the early afternoon sun was not too strong, I was still sweaty by the time I arrived at the police station. I looked longingly at the café across the street—what I wouldn't do for a cappuccino—but regrettably turned away. I had no money. And now no job.

Thank goodness for Auntie Akamai.

I started across the street to my destination and was almost to the door when it opened and out came Ainsley. When she saw me, she glanced left and right, looking like a cornered animal. She was clearly not happy to see me.

And neither was the woman following her, who was so close behind her that she ran into her when Ainsley saw me. "Ainsley, what is your problem. Walk," she said, giving her a little shove.

I knew it was her mother immediately because the two of them looked so much alike there wasn't much doubt that they were related, or at least had the same plastic surgeon. They both had bleached blonde hair, long limbs with zero cellulite and practically identical nose jobs, and the same penchant for scanty clothing. The biggest difference between them was her mother carried herself in perpetual come-hither mode, while Ainsley managed to radiate youth and innocence.

"Mom," whispered Ainsley, inclining her head to me. As if I couldn't hear or see them.

"Oh, so there's the little murderess now," said Ainsley's mother in an overly loud voice. Several people passing by gawked at me.

"Mom, stop!" Ainsley elbowed her mother. I couldn't for the life of me remember her mother's name. I just got the image of a snake, its tongue darting out at me.

"Well," continued her mother, "she seems to be turning

herself in, which is good." She stopped in front of me, looking me up and down critically. "They'll be a little more lenient with your sentence if you're cooperative." She turned halfway to Ainsley. "You're right, Ainsley. She will look horrid in orange."

I stood there, mouth hanging open as I looked from mother to daughter. "Excuse me?" I finally managed to sputter.

"Why did you run away from home, dear?" Ainsley's mother continued in her overly loud voice. "Did you get caught stealing from your parents again? Or caught with drugs this time?"

Anger surged through me, and I could feel my face turning red. "What in the world are you talking about?" I hissed the words, my fists tightening.

A slippery smile curved her lips. "The girls told us all about your record at school, dearest. My only surprise is you haven't gone to jail yet." She looked me up and down again, laughing at my casual attire. "Or have you? The girls haven't seen you in a few years."

I was shaking now, but not sure if it was anger or fear. "You're making things up," I said as loudly as I could manage. "You're lying."

Ainsley danced back and forth from foot to foot. "Mom, let's go." She whined and tugged at her mother, trying to pull her away. She mouthed *I'm sorry*, I think.

What is she sorry for? Her mother's behavior or… *Oh no*. My stomach turned. They must have been here at the station to tell those lies to the police.

Ainsley's mother laughed, and then suddenly she arranged her features like she was posing for a camera.

Because she was.

That woman from the parking lot yesterday, the reporter, stood in the street, right off the curb. She held up her cell phone, videoing us. I turned away and hurried to the door of the police station and ran smack into Detective Ray as he walked out. But he wasn't looking at me.

"Miss Chase," he shouted.

"I'm in public space, Detective," she laughed, pointing at the curb with her free hand. "Not on your precious sidewalk."

Detective Ray didn't look at me as he passed. "Ladies,"

he said to Ainsley and her mother, "please move along." Then he turned to the reporter. "Miss Chase…"

But before he could finish his sentence, she waved him off. "I know, I know…don't harass the resort guests." She laughed and slipped her phone into a bag slung across her body. She shot me a crocodile smile. "She's not a resort guest anymore though," she tossed over her shoulder as she sauntered off.

I watched her go, wondering what all she got on video.

CHAPTER ELEVEN

———

Across the table, Detective Ray watched me as I squirmed. The back of my legs stuck to the cheap chairs, and I imagined there would be a Velcro sound when I stood up to leave.

If I was allowed to stand up and leave.

My assumption about Ainsley and her mother was correct. They had told Detective Ray all kinds of stories and assured him I had no record because my parents paid off crooked New York policemen. A multitude of crimes swept under a rug by dollar bills.

I told him five hundred times that they're all lies. The only thing I'd ever been in trouble for was wearing my school uniform blouse untucked at my all-girl's middle school.

I even told him that.

He just watched me with his dark eyes impressively blank.

A uniformed policewoman came in to take a hair sample. I yanked a few out on my own.

"Can I go now?"

Detective Ray watched me for a moment more, then nodded, still silent.

I stood and fled. Back out on the street, I glanced up and down to make sure the reporter woman was not around. I didn't see her, so I hurried away, back to the resort. I hoped she wasn't allowed to be there like Auntie Akamai said.

I found a bench in the shade and sat to think.

I hadn't mentioned to the detective I thought Ainsley and the others were connected to the dead man. How could I without implicating myself in breaking and entering Joey's room?

But, I realized, at least he now knew about them. They

had basically offered themselves up as additional suspects while trying to make me look like a huge criminal, which in itself must have looked suspicious, right? And apparently, we had all arrived the same day, albeit on different flights, so it wasn't out of the realm of possibility that he had followed them here, and just happened upon me. Well, except that he had told me he had been following me for weeks... I spun my hair around my finger as I thought through the facts.

If the police had found the codes, they would be working to decipher them too. They had to have found them, since the code sheet was lying right under the desk now, thanks to my blunder. Right?

I pulled out my phone and studied the lines of code yet again. If they were dollar amounts, what did they mean? And what did the rest of the letters stand for? *TE*? *CC*? *S&T*?

I leaned back and stared at the tree across from me. I had to figure this out to get the detective off my back. Right now it was gibberish. I didn't even know for sure the letters were initials, but it was a mighty big coincidence if they weren't.

My mind wandered back to the last set of initials. *SJ*. Who is *SJ*? I whispered the letters aloud. I did it repeatedly and slowed the letters down as my brain fried from the sheer effort of thinking. "Esssssssss..."

A staff member passed me and gave me a sideways glance before she hurried off. She must have thought I'm crazy, sitting here hissing at myself. I laughed.

Wait a sec.

Hissing.

S is for snake.

That's why I could only came up with the image of a snake when Ainsley's mother was talking to me. Her name starts with an *S*! I'm sure of it! I sat up in my excitement, then immediately crumpled back down.

Rickenbacker didn't start with a *J*. Not even a silent one. So though Ainsley's mother might be a snake, she wasn't *SJ*.

I sat there with terrible posture when the daughter of the snake walked by.

Ainsley hesitated, then stopped. Wringing her hands, she looked down at me.

I glared.

"Can I make it up to you?" she asked meekly.

"Make it up to me? For going to the police and telling them I'm a murderer, making up lies?" I arched my eyebrows at her, channeling the unflappable Mrs. Barrington the best I could, and managing to keep my cool.

"Ned and I are going sailing. Come along and I'll explain it to you, okay?" Her blue eyes pleaded with me.

Well, I didn't have anything else to do. And this would give me an excellent excuse to ask some questions. Maybe I could figure out what their codes meant. She denied knowing Joey before, but maybe she would explain herself now.

Plus, it would give me a ride to the Aloha Lagoon Marina. It's safe to assume the murderer—or murderers—took Joey to the lava tubes in a boat. Maybe there would be some clues there.

"Can we drop by where I'm staying to change clothes?" I asked. "I have more appropriate clothes for sailing." I remembered too late they would see my shack, but the horse was already out of the gate and Ainsley was riding it for all it's worth.

"Sure, of course. I didn't realize you weren't here at the resort," she gushed, yapping away. It occurred to me now that Claire probably didn't want to hang out with her, so she was probably lonely for girl chat.

Lucky me.

She pulled me off the bench and dragged me along to the front of the hotel, where Ned was waiting in a car. Annoyance flashed over his face until he saw how happy Ainsley was. I wondered idly if he had ever made Heather, his now ex-wife, that happy at any time during their marriage.

Of course, she may be plenty happy now with the alimony Claire had mentioned.

I gave him directions to Auntie Akamai's and wondered the whole five minute drive how to explain that I lived in the equivalent of a screened-in porch.

In the end, Paulie saved me. Auntie Akamai was sitting on her lawn with a friend, and Paulie was on the back of her chair. As soon as Ainsley saw him, she didn't see anything else. I told Auntie Akamai I just came to change, and she didn't bat an eye when I went into the house…and out the other side.

In my room I pulled the suitcase from under the bed and shuffled through it quickly, finding a designer top and capris, as well as my usual boating shoes. I ran a brush through my hair and braided it, then dabbed a little lip gloss on. I didn't feel like doing the whole makeup routine I would have back in the city. Who was going to see me besides my hosts?

Minutes later, we arrived at the Aloha Lagoon Marina. The dive shop's boat, the *Mahina*, was not moored, so they must have been out on a dive.

"Turn your frown upside down, Katherine!" Ainsley pulled me into a suffocating hug. "This will be a ton of fun!"

She released me and bounded down the dock. Ned watched her, smiling.

"After you." He gestured.

As I walked down the dock, I looked carefully at the boats. Like there was going to be a big splash of blood on one of them, or Joey's wallet.

Once we were all on board, Ned steered the sailboat out using the motor. As we passed the end of the marina where the boats were the size of the dingy on my parent's yacht, I heard raised voices. Two men yelled back and forth, while a third hurried down the dock to intervene.

"You stole my boat!" a tall man hollered at a shorter one.

"No, I didn't!" The shorter one looked ready to fight.

"Then why is it in your slip!"

"I told you, I don't know! This is the first time I've been here this week!"

I strained to hear more, but distance and Ainsley made it impossible.

"Ugh, for real. So classy." She rolled her eyes at the arguing men as they became gesticulating ants on the dock.

A different thought had crossed my mind.

Ainsley sat on the padded bench and gestured to me to sit as well. "So what do you think of Ned?" She blushed and smiled over her shoulder at him, and they exchanged air-blown kisses.

Geesh. "Um…" I looked at my shoes. "I was pretty surprised, to be honest."

I glanced up to see her nodding sagely. "Of course, sure. I was surprised by it myself."

I tried my best to keep the disgusted look off my face. There was literally nothing I wanted to know about how they got together. It was just so *ick*. Ainsley had been his daughter's best friend since elementary school! I casted around for something, anything to change the subject to.

"Is there a bathroom on this boat?"

She nodded and pointed toward the cabin door.

I descended into the boat's small cabin and headed toward where the facilities were probably located. I found the bathroom but, unfortunately, also the bedroom. The bed was clearly used, as it was unmade, the sheets strewn around and pillows askew.

I was so grossed out I almost turned around and went back up, but I actually did need to use the bathroom now.

When I emerged back on the deck, I almost turned around and went back down. The couple were entwined, giggling and kissing loudly.

I gave a polite cough and whispered an apology before spying a nautical map on the desk. I put all my attention on it and tried to block out the smooching sounds. Using what Kahiau taught me, I oriented myself and found the marina, then searched for the lava tubes.

"You like maps?" Ned came up next to me. "Or looking for something specific?"

I straightened. "Just looking."

He leaned over and studied the map, tracing a route with his manicured finger. "This is where we'll go this afternoon. Around here, to here, then back." He looked down at me. "Sound good?"

I nodded. He kept some pretty intense eye contact, and it felt weird. Especially when I realized he had the same green eyes as his son and daughter. I joined Ainsley on the padded bench again.

She smiled at me blandly. "Sorry about that. We just can't help it."

I ignored that and stared her in the eye. She had nowhere to run, and Ned wasn't paying us any attention right now. "What was the deal with your mother?"

Ainsley fidgeted and looked away. I think she now realized what her need for female companionship had gotten her. She sighed and tried in vain to capture her long blonde locks as they were tossed around by the wind.

"She's just being a mom," she finally said. "She thinks she's protecting me."

"By throwing me under the bus? Nice." I watched her for a beat before adding, "What's your mom's name again?"

"Susan." Ainsley gave me a funny look.

Ah, that's right. The S name. But what about the J... "Wait. Why would you need protecting?"

She shot a pleading look at Ned, but he didn't notice, and the wind had carried away our words. "We knew the guy who drowned."

"You mean the guy who was murdered?" It was spiteful, but I was curious to see her reaction. "The one you previously denied knowing?"

Her face drained of color, making her full face of "natural" makeup look like a clown face. "Yes," she whispered, barely loud enough to hear, "and Mom thinks Ned might have done it."

CHAPTER TWELVE

"Ladies," Ned boomed, "let's put up the sails!"

Nice timing, Ned.

I attempted to grab Ainsley's hand, but she got up in a flash. "Coming, babe!" she called out to Ned.

I stood too but was uncertain what to do. I didn't know much about sailing, but I did know to keep clear of the boom, the bottom arm of the large sail which swung around to catch the wind.

Then something caught my eye, poking out between the bench and a storage bin. It looked like a mesh bag, the kind you take diving to collect things in. I stepped over to it and bent down to see…a bag of diving weights.

Just like the ones that were stolen from the dive shop.

Just like the ones that were used to drown Joey.

I stared at them. Could it be a coincidence? Ainsley admitted her mom suspected Ned, and now here were some dive weights. But there could be a number of reasons to have dive weights. Right?

But none I could think of off the top of my head. Except for weighing down bodies, of course. And not in a diving way. People didn't usually go diving from a sailboat.

I heard my name being called and straightened. As I turned, I saw something coming at me, and coming at me fast! I threw up my arms to protect my face, and they took the brunt of the swinging boom, but it was still going fast enough and was heavy enough to knock me clear off the boat.

I hit the water head first and was stunned for a moment, then fought my way to the surface and burst out, gasping. I heard Ainsley screaming, and as I treaded water, I looked up at the two faces staring down.

"Are you okay?" Ned called down to me. His head disappeared for a moment, then popped back over with a life ring buoy in his hand.

I waved it off and started to swim to the back of the boat.

"Bring her up, baby! There might be sharks!" Ainsley shrieked.

There was a little ladder at the stern, and I grabbed hold of the bottom rung.

What if it had been intentional?

If I got back on this boat, might they try again?

I couldn't see the panicked Ainsley as a murderer. But the face peering down at me…even his future mother-in-law had doubts. And surely she knew him better than I did.

"Do you need help up?" he called down. His face looked appropriately concerned.

I knew I was grasping at straws. I started to pull myself up the ladder. Until I could get a foothold, it was purely arm strength, which told me for sure that people did not dive from this boat. There was no way I could have climbed out with all the equipment on. As it was, Ned grasped my hand and hauled me out.

He helped me to the bench and squatted in front of me, Ainsley hovering behind him flapping her hands. "Why did you stand up?" she whined at me. "I was telling you to stay down."

I shook my head. "I only heard my name. I didn't hear anything else."

"Did it hit you in the head?" Ned asked, straightening his legs enough to check my head.

"No, I put my arms up." I held them up to show the bruises already blooming on my forearms. Typical self-defense wounds, according to every police drama ever.

"Oh, ouch." Ned took an arm gently and looked at it. "I hope nothing is broken."

"I think I'm fine." I pulled my arms away and wrapped them around my torso. "They don't hurt too bad."

Um, yeah, they did. I just didn't want him touching me.

"Oh," wailed Ainsley, still in freak-out mode. "Your clothes! And that's Fendi, isn't it?"

I looked down at my soaked outfit. It wasn't, but I wasn't

about to admit it. "Do you have a towel?"

Ainsley nodded and hurried away.

No, wait. Don't leave me alone with Ned...

"You sure you're okay?" He made the uncomfortable eye contact again. "Do you want to head back, or change into some of Ainsley's clothes and stick with the plan?"

Ainsley returned with a fluffy towel. "Oh, your shoes," she fussed.

"Do you have anything here for her to wear?" Ned looked at her.

She shook her head. "Only my sunbathing...bottoms."

Ned sent her a mischievous smile then turned back to me. "I may have a shirt?"

I took a break from drying my hair to wave his suggestion off. "I'm fine. It will be fine."

He stayed where he was, crouching by my knees so he could look at me at eye level. "You sure?" I noticed again that his sandy blond hair had a few grays running through it, and not just at his temples.

After I nodded, he stood, and I wrapped the towel around me. I pulled my shoes off and set them in the sun to dry. Ainsley glanced down at them. "Oh, good. They're cheap."

"They're also very comfortable and have good grip for boat decks." I looked pointedly at her four-inch heels, which probably cost more than the rent I would owe Auntie Akamai.

She followed my gaze to her own shoes.

"I might have a death wish, but I'd like to continue our conversation," I said in a low voice. Ned had moved off to secure the boom and hopefully wouldn't hear us.

"Thank goodness you weren't wearing makeup." She smiled weakly.

"Not that conversation." I arched my eyebrows. "You owe me now."

Her shoulders slumped. She sat down next to me, careful to not sit in the puddle I had formed. "Yes, we knew him. Vaguely, but knew him."

"How?"

She pursed her lips and shot a glance at Ned. "He was hired by Ned's ex-wife."

"Heather? Why?" I glanced at Ned to make sure he was still out of earshot. I also thought it odd that she referred to Heather as simply the ex-wife and not her former BFF's mom.

She had the decency to blush. "When we, um, you know. Got together. She hired Joey to follow Ned around until he caught us together."

I didn't really care to hear the details. "So if it weren't for him...you wouldn't have been caught?"

"Oh, no." She waved her hands in front of her. "He was going to leave her for me anyway. We had plans to get married. He was waiting for the right time to divorce her."

I stared at her. I knew she wasn't the most book smart woman, but apparently not common sense smart either. That was the oldest line in the book. But okay. "But the alimony wouldn't be as high, probably, if it was just a normal divorce without proven infidelity."

She checked behind her again to make sure Ned was out of hearing range. "I dunno. But when Ned saw Joey here in Aloha Lagoon, he thought maybe he was still following him."

I frowned. "Why would he be?"

She shrugged. "But then you said he was here for you, so we knew that wasn't the case. It was a super weird coincidence."

"Okay. But what are those dive weights doing here? You don't dive." I pointed to the end of the bench.

Ainsley swiveled to look, and her movement caught Ned's attention. He came over to see what she was looking at.

"What are those, babe?" Ainsley pointed. "Katherine says they're dive weights."

Ned squatted to look at them but didn't reach out a hand. "Looks like they are indeed." He glanced up at me. "Dive weights are how the body was disposed of, aren't they?"

The back of my neck prickled. "How would I know?"

He straightened, standing to his full height, and crossed his arms. "They said you were the one who found him."

"Well, yeah, but I didn't know what was holding him on the ocean floor. The detective told me they were dive weights."

Ned studied me for a long minute, then looked back at the weights. "Well, I've never seen them before." And in one fluid motion, he bent, picked up the bag, and chucked it over the side of the boat.

"Wait!" I bolted to my feet, shocked. "They could be evidence! They could have the murderer's fingerprints!"

"Yup." He wiped his hands together and looked down at us with a Cheshire Cat grin. "Ainsley and I are each other's alibi. They have no evidence either way, and I am not going to take the fall for something I didn't do."

I stood, backed up a few steps, and looked toward shore. *Could I swim that far?*

Ned started laughing. "Oh, I didn't mean it like that. I'm not saying we did anything. Don't look so scared."

When I didn't move, he gestured at the island. "Do you want to go back? I can drop you off if you're not comfortable." He looked me up and down. "Physically or mentally."

* * *

As I stood on the dock, my clothes dripped onto the wooden boards. I looked toward the boat the men were arguing about earlier. It wouldn't hurt to take a look, right?

I walked up the dock toward the shore and was about to turn onto the next dock when a voice called out to me.

"Excuse me. Excuse me, Miss Barrington?"

I turned to see that blasted reporter waving me down.

"Do you have a moment?" She put out a hand when she reached me but didn't attempt to touch me.

I crossed my arms. "What do you want?"

"I'm looking for a scoop on the big wedding, and I see you're friends with the blushing bride." She tipped her head and looked at me. "Do you know where it's being held?"

"No, not a clue. I wasn't invited." I scowled at her. "It was just a coincidence I'm here."

"So you do know Miss Rickenbacker and Mr. D'Angelo." She beamed at me like she had caught me.

"Well, obviously." I gestured at the boat disappearing into the distance.

"What is your relationship with the slick tax avoider and his vapid child bride?" She made air quotes around *avoider* and smiled, showing her teeth.

"Huh? What are you talking about? She's not a child. She's twenty-two!"

"And you are friends with Miss Jameson too?"

"Who?"

She waved away the question and decided to go for the harder hitting ones, apparently. "What do you know about the murder?"

"Nothing," I said.

"The police seem to think you do." Her hand started to go to her pocket, then stopped. "I've seen them talking to you multiple times now."

I shook my head, but she persisted.

"What is your connection to Joseph Morton?"

The sound of an approaching motorcycle made us both turn. As it approached, the reporter's hand went to her pocket again, and this time she pulled out her phone.

The bike roared right up to us at the edge of the dock, and Dex grinned from the seat. "Want a ride?"

"Yes," I said and practically ran to him. I threw my leg over and grabbed him. "Go!" I whispered.

"Your wish is my command," he said, and we were off on his noble steed.

CHAPTER THIRTEEN

———

Dex pulled into the dive shop lot and stopped and turned off the bike.

I have to admit I enjoyed hanging on to his body for dear life, so it was disappointing to already have arrived.

I climbed off the back of the bike and feebly swiped at the seat. "Thank you for the rescue." I remembered, now that I was face-to-face with him, that our last meeting had ended on a bad note.

"I saw a damsel in distress." He winked at me. "I happened to be driving by, coming back to work from home." He looked me up and down, but not in a creepy way. "Wait. What happened to you?"

"I fell off a sailboat." I shrugged. "Well, actually knocked off by the boom."

"What? Are you okay?" He noticed my arms and took one, gently, and turned it to see the bruises. "Wow."

"Yeah." I pulled my arm back. "I don't really know how it happened—accident or not—but I'm fine."

He frowned. "You think it wasn't an accident?"

"I don't know. Maybe I'm overreacting with all this murder business." I looked down at my wet clothes. "I had better get on back to my place to change." The sun was already drying my clothes, but I shivered.

"Do you want a ride the rest of the way?"

I shook my head. "No, I'm fine. Let the sun and wind dry me a little more as I walk." I gave him a big fake smile and waved. "Thanks again for the rescue."

I turned and started off, but he trotted alongside me until I stopped.

"Hey, do you want to try that Spam restaurant tonight?"

He smiled, reminding me of those nice teeth.

A rush of warmth went through me. "Sure."

"Six thirty?" He raised his eyebrows, waiting.

"Yes, I think that would be good. Give me a chance to clean up and dry off." I smiled and gave him a little wave. "See you then."

I was giddy and wanted to do nothing more than daydream about dinner with Dex, but I needed to think over what had happened on the boat and about what the reporter had said.

Was the boom accident really an accident? And why did he throw the weights off the boat? Should I tell Detective Ray?

And what did the reporter mean by "tax avoider"? Is that even a thing?

I rolled my eyes, annoyed afresh by her comment about Ainsley being a child bride. I mean, yes, she is the same age as his daughter, but she's not a child.

Speaking of his daughter, I looked up to see her walking toward me on the beach. She was kicking the water and smiling, but probably just because she hadn't seen me yet.

"Hey, Claire." I waved at her, relishing in her initial expression of shock.

Her step faltered a bit, but she kept her smile pasted on. "Hey."

"What are you doing out here?" I noticed she was wearing a backpack that looked pretty full. "Hiking?"

She made a face, then laughed. "Oh, yeah. Hiking. I had to get away from the fam, you know?" She looked away like she was searching for a subject. "And what are you doing out here?"

I nodded with my chin. "I'm staying in a house out here."

"Hmm." She kept looking away. "Okay then, well, be seeing you."

"Yeah, okay." I watched her walk away, no longer playing in the surf but walking like she had somewhere to be. She always was a bit weird.

When I got back to the house, Auntie Akamai had a cow about my soaked appearance and bruises. She wanted to run to the police that very minute. I had no interest in going back anytime soon if I could help it.

"Actually…" I pulled my arms back from her gentle

hands. "I wanted to know what to wear to the Spam restaurant."

"Sir Spamalot's?" She eyed me. "Just shorts and T-shirt is fine. This is Hawaii, girlie. But dry clothes are probably a good idea."

I laughed and circled my hand around my face. "I need to shower, so yes, I will put on dry clothes."

When I came out of the shower, I could hear Paulie cursing a blue streak. Dex must have arrived. He and Auntie Akamai were on the front porch, Dex's neck bright red.

"Well," he said, "I was telling Kiki about Spam—she had never had it before. So I was coming by to take her to Sir Spamalot's."

Auntie Akamai's eyebrows rose, but she smiled. "Okay. You two enjoy."

Dex and I stood staring at each other stupidly.

"Well, go on, you two." Auntie Akamai flapped her hands at us but had a twinkle in her eye.

Dex led me out to the motorcycle. "I hope this is okay? I use my dad's jeep when there's something I need to carry, but this is mine for zipping around."

I nodded. "Sure."

After a short but exhilarating drive, Dex pulled into a parking lot. Ahead of us was an open-air eatery lit with strings of lights swaying in the breeze, giving them a twinkly appearance. I followed Dex to a table, where he and the waiter did a cool-dude handshake before pulling out the rickety chair for me. Stained paper menus were under a ketchup bottle.

I couldn't help but smile to myself. My mother would be absolutely horrified.

"So do you have a recommendation?" I pulled a menu sheet to me and glanced down it.

"Well, a traditional favorite is Spam Musubi. It's like Spam sushi."

"Okay." I looked across at him, my head tipped to the side. "If I don't care for it, you can finish it?"

He laughed. "Sure."

We ordered, our sodas coming in cans that weren't completely cold. Again, Mrs. Barrington would lose her mind.

But *Miss* Barrington thoroughly enjoyed herself. The

meat (if you call it meat?) was salty, the dinner companion sweet.

Until he decided to ask personal questions.

"So, are you going to tell me how you know those girls from the bar? One was on the dive trip." He folded his hands across his stomach and leaned back.

I frowned. "Claire D'Angelo and her mother were on the dive trip. Ainsley Rickenbacker was in the bar with her fiancé, Ned D'Angelo."

His head tipped, making him look like a cute puppy. "Is D'Angelo a really common name, or is Ainsley's fiancé Claire's brother?"

I couldn't help but smile at the expected reaction to the news that was to come. "No, Ned is not Claire's brother. He is her *father*." I let it sink in, loving the expression on his face. "Exactly," I told him. "To make things even weirder, Ainsley did date Claire's brother, plus she and Claire were best friends in school."

His mouth opened and closed like a fish. I knew he was trying to find a way to ask any of the multitude of questions that had gone through my head when I'd found out.

Finally, with a pained look on his face, he sat forward. "So the mom on the dive trip is the ex-wife?"

I nodded.

"Recent or old news?"

"Recent enough that I had no idea. Ainsley told me this afternoon that the divorce came after she and Ned were caught together. And you want to know who caught them? Who provided the evidence to Mrs. D'Angelo?"

He ran a hand down his face. "I'm not sure I want to know, but who?"

"Joey Morton. The Sea Urchin."

Dex threw himself back in the chair and looked from side to side. Then he leaned forward conspiratorially. "Are you serious?"

I nodded as I reached for my soda. "And today, not only was I 'accidentally' knocked overboard after Ainsley told me, but I also watched as Ned dropped a bag of dive weights off the side of the boat."

Dex frowned. "Our dive weights?" Then he shook his head. "So they stole the dive weights? Those rich people?" He blushed then hurried on. "Do you think Ainsley is strong enough to suffocate Joey? Or maybe she distracted him while Ned did, then they dragged him off together to the boat…"

"Suffocated?" Detective Ray had said Joey didn't drown, but how did Dex know?

He nodded. "The bag over his head. The weights were to make him disappear. Or worse, the bag rendered him unconscious and the weights caused him to drown."

Oh goodness.

I looked down at the remains of the Spam sushi, and my stomach rolled.

"How did you know he was suffocated?" I asked.

Dex's eyes darted around. "I heard it somewhere. You hadn't heard?"

I shook my head.

"Well, back to my original question…how did you know them all?"

Was he trying to distract me?

"We went to the same all-girls prep school." I dabbed my mouth with my napkin, hoping the sour feeling in my stomach would pass.

"Prep? What's that mean?" Dex picked at the tiny remnants of his food.

"Preparatory. It's high school…for rich kids." I felt the heat in my face again and looked away.

"Ah."

"Then we went off to our separate colleges. I haven't seen them since our high school graduation." I took a tentative sip of my drink, experimenting to see how it would feel going down.

"What did you study in college?" Dex leaned back and crossed his arms, his feet bumping mine as he did the same with his legs.

The familiar anger began to bubble up inside. "Well, if my mother had her choice, I would have just gotten my MRS degree."

Dex's eyebrows went together. "MRS? Masters?"

"No," I snorted. "Like missus. Found a rich husband. Which is all she thinks I'm good for. Making 'a good match' as she would say." I looked away, surprised by the flash of anger that warmed my neck.

Dex seemed surprised by it too and made an "ah" sound.

"But..." I leaned forward and planted my elbows on the table in defiance of my upbringing. "I wanted to actually learn something."

He leaned forward. "So...what did you study?"

"Marine biology."

His head bobbed forward. "Wow! Really? That's very cool."

I smiled and blushed, for a *good* reason this time.

"So you could definitely be leading the tours." He pointed at me. "Or you could teach some identification classes before the dives."

I laughed. "No, I'm no expert."

I realized we were grinning at each other like complete dorks.

"Can I ask you one more very deep, personal question?" Dex leaned forward again.

"I might regret this, but sure." I made a "go on" motion with my hand.

"What is your actual name?"

I frowned at him. "But you know it. It's in the logbook." I waited a moment for him to confirm or deny, but since he didn't, I went on. "Let me explain that my mother really likes Tiffany's."

"The jewelry store?"

"Yes, definitely the store, but also the movie *Breakfast at Tiffany's*."

"Oh." Dex frowned. "You know, I have no idea what it's about. I used to think it was about eating breakfast at some girl named Tiffany's house."

I couldn't help but giggle, but he didn't look offended. Instead, his face lit up at the sound.

I continued. "It was a book first. Then a movie in the sixties starring Katherine Hepburn."

"Okay...so there's the Hepburn."

"Yes. Well, my given name at birth was…" I took a deep breath and said it as regally as I could muster. "Katherine Tiffany Barrington."

"Okay, Katherine like Katherine Hepburn." I nodded, so he continued. "What's Kiki?"

"Oh, that's just a nickname my nanny gave me." I smiled at the memory of the sweet old lady.

"Oh." Dex looked uncomfortable again. "You had a nanny?"

"Well, a housekeeper and various babysitters, sure, but I was referring to my grandmother." I wanted to laugh at his assumption, but that wouldn't be very nice. "But I liked it and used it in college. Simply another way to horrify my mother." I looked away over the short wall and watched a taxi pull up.

"What's the deal with you and your parents?" Dex said.

I sighed, looking back at him. "You said one more personal question."

He gave me a cute and kind smile. "Okay. I guess that can be enough sharing for now."

"You could tell me something about you instead." I gestured at him, and he reached his hand out too. *He wants to hold my hand?*

"Like what? I'm boring." He put his hand on the edge of his plate like that's what he was reaching for.

But before I could formulate a question, a flash blinded us.

CHAPTER FOURTEEN

———

Surprised by the camera flash, my reaction was to shield my face. But then I realized it wasn't pointed at me.

It was Felicity Chase, but her prey was a tall, leggy blonde who waltzed into the place like she owned it, a man in a suit following her like a little puppy.

"Oh," the woman said loudly, her long blonde hair swinging left and right as she walked by our table. "How *quaint.*"

Dex tapped my hand and gestured for me to come closer.

"Does that voice sound familiar to you?" He inclined his head slightly toward the woman, who was now going on about humble trappings and getting to know the locals.

I closed my eyes and listened. Yes, *definitely.*

It was Susan, Ainsley's mother.

I nodded and opened my eyes. I darted my eyes to her to make sure she didn't see us and leaned forward. "It's Ainsley's mother."

He frowned. "Really?"

I nodded. "And I'd really like to leave before she sees me. She made a huge scene in front of the police station this morning, yelling accusations at me. It was awful." I blinked my stupid eyes as they filled with tears. "Plus that reporter is here again."

"Actually I was thinking her voice sounded like the woman we heard arguing when I walked you to your room. Remember?" He was leaning forward too, and his eyes were filled with concern.

I took a calming breath and closed my eyes, listening again.

"I think you might be right," I said, my eyes still closed.

"The voice did say something about Ainsley."

I jumped back when a rough thumb touched my cheek, lifting off a tear that had escaped. I opened my eyes to see him peering at me with a weird look on his face.

I scowled at him. "I've had a rough day, okay? I was accosted by her." I nudged my chin toward Susan. "Then knocked off a boat, and then interrogated by the reporter." I glanced around. "Maybe it's time to go. I don't see the reporter anymore."

"Wait just a second," he said, holding out his hand. "Didn't you say Ainsley's last name was Rocken-something?"

"Rickenbacker."

"Well, Felicity Chase called her 'Miss Jameson.'"

I stared at him. "She asked me how I knew a Miss Jameson earlier. I had no idea who she was talking about. Why is she calling her that?"

Somewhere from the recesses of my brain, the letters *S* and *J* floated up. The initials *SJ*.

Susan Jameson. Jameson must be her maiden name.

I gasped. "Oh my!"

"What?" he asked, his head whipping around. "Is Felicity Chase back? I thought I saw the owner escort her out."

"No, I just realized something. But I need to confirm it first. Can you take me back to Auntie Akamai's now?"

His face fell. "I thought we could walk out on the Pier."

"Oh." I squirmed in my seat. "Maybe another night? Or tomorrow afternoon? I do want to go with you, but I need to take care of something right now."

Dex nodded but didn't make eye contact. "Yeah, sure."

I reached out a hand to touch one of his. "Tomorrow afternoon?"

"Sure."

Wow. Moody much?

"Okay." My stomach churned as I watched him reach for his back pocket. It hadn't even crossed my mind until now. *I am a charity case.*

His eyes met mine, and he shook his head. "Don't worry about it. I got it."

* * *

Dex dropped me off at the curb and then roared off into the night. I moped my way up to Auntie Akamai's door and raised my hand to knock on the edge of the screen door's wooden frame.

"Knock, knock," Paulie squawked before my knuckles even made contact.

"Better than a doorbell, this one." Auntie Akamai's voice came through the door. "Come on in, girlie."

"Giiiiiiiiiirrrrrleeeeee," called Paulie.

"Thanks." I opened the door and found the eternally happy woman sitting in a recliner in front of the TV, watching a show with a man with a huge seventies-style mustache.

"Oh, I love Magnum," she sighed.

I took a seat on a bamboo-print loveseat and crossed my legs at the ankles, like a lady. "So, I have got an update."

I ran through the day, from being accosted by Susan in front of the police station, to the disastrous boat trip and being interrogated by the reporter. "And then, at dinner, Susan showed up and Dex recognized her voice and the reporter called her—get this: 'Miss Jameson.'"

Auntie Akamai sat forward, the footrest slamming shut. "Susan Jameson. *SJ*!"

I laughed. "Wow, you got that fast."

She actually *giggled* as she wiggled forward until she could lever herself out of the chair. "Let's goggle her."

I smiled and whispered, "Google." She was already out of the room, so she probably hadn't heard me correct her, but Paulie did.

"Google!" He bobbed his head and swayed his body from side to side. "*Google*!"

"Shhhh," I whispered, waving a hand at him. "Don't be embarrassing."

Auntie Akamai came back in, carrying her laptop. She sat next to me, propping it open on her lap, and typed in the password before handing it to me.

I opened the internet and typed in *Susan Jameson New York.* The screen filled with images of the lean blonde galivanting around the city, attending fundraisers, fancy functions, or walking on the street. I scrolled down, and article after non-news article featured a picture of her.

"Well, she's classy." Auntie Akamai snorted. "Do you see a common theme with these pictures?"

I scrolled back up, giving them a second look. Never the same dress and...

"Never the same man." Auntie Akamai voiced my thought. "She's a..."

"Socialite." I nodded.

"*Hussy!*" Paulie screamed, winning a scowl from his owner.

"Oh shush, you rotten chicken!" Auntie Akamai started to stand, but Paulie took to the air and flapped into the next room.

"Chicken," he called out from the other room.

"Always with the last word, that one," Auntie Akamai muttered as she eased herself back down onto the loveseat. "Okay, so where's the dirt on her, other than she is a 'socialite.' Do you know anything about Ainsley's father? Was he one of these men?"

I scrolled down the page again until we came to photos taken decades ago. There we found her, fresh face framed with big, poufy curls, sitting next to an old man. She had her hand on his arm and was gazing at him with adoration. I pointed at it.

"What?" Auntie Akamai stared. "Please tell me that's her grandfather."

"Nope. He's Mr. Rickenbacker."

"Ainsley's father?" Auntie Akamai's mouth hung open. "Seriously? He looks like the Crypt Keeper."

"I know. I always wondered how Ainsley came to be, if you know what I mean." I pointed at another picture. "This one was in her dorm room. She idolized him, thought he was bigger than life, even though he died when she was two or three."

"That's rough." Auntie Akamai shook her head. "Growing up without a father, seeing her mother going out with all these other men." She waved her hand dismissively. "No wonder she is marrying her best friend's father."

On a whim, I pulled up the Wikipedia page on Mr.

Rickenbacker. "It looks like Susan was his fourth wife!"

Auntie Akamai touched her screen. "Look at the marriage date versus his date of death."

"What's that, like three or four months?" I gaped at the screen, then scrolled down to the paragraph on the marriage. While the first three had wedding pictures, Susan's paragraph did not and only consisted of a few lines of text. On the bottom of the page were links to various articles. We scanned through a few, finding references to all of his marriages and wives except for Susan.

Moving on, I remembered what the reporter had said about Ned. I typed in "tax avoidance." A definition was at the top of the search results. *Tax Avoidance: The careful arrangement of financial affairs to minimize tax liability within the law. Compare with* tax evasion.

"Tax avoidance versus tax evasion." Auntie Akamai squinted at the screen. "Why are you looking at this?"

"Just something the reporter said." I shrugged.

"Felicity?" Auntie Akamai grunted and leaned back, folding her arms. "Don't listen to anything that woman says. Don't worry about her."

CHAPTER FIFTEEN

———

That attitude certainly changed the next morning when Auntie Akamai burst through my door, waving a newspaper. "Kiki!"

I bolted upright from a lovely dream starring a certain handsome Hawaiian man. "Who-what?" I wiped drool off my chin with the back of my hand.

"Felicity Chase, that woman, wrote about you!" She spit the words out angrily as she waved the paper furiously in the air.

"*What?!*" I bolted out of the small bed and over to where she was spreading the newspaper on the table. There on pages five and six was an article accompanied by several pictures.

"Look at the headline! *The Heiress in the Shack!* Can you believe it? This isn't a *shack*! It's a…" She glared around us. "A lanai. A furnished lanai."

The secondary headline read *NYC-style Crime Follows Affluent Family to Aloha Lagoon.*

"Oh no," I moaned, sitting in the chair and dropping my chin into my hands. "Does anyone actually read this paper?"

Auntie Akamai straightened and glared. "Yes, girl. This is the *Aloha Sun*. It's our local paper."

"I didn't mean to offend you." I grimaced. "I meant more do the articles get picked up by the AP? The Associated Press newswire?"

"I know what the AP is." Auntie Akamai shrugged. "I don't know if they do."

"I'm only wondering if my parents will see it." I leaned over the newspaper again. There were photos of the "furnished lanai" that I lived in, the coroner's van, the dive shop, Ned and Ainsley on the sailboat, Susan posing in front of the police station, and Dex and me at dinner. "Oh man."

"I am calling the editor right now. This is *not* a shack." Auntie Akamai stormed off, leaving the paper behind.

I read the article, blushing when I read a comment about Dex and "love blooming on the Garden Isle" and banging my fist on the table when it inferred I had been arrested for murder. The article did outline quite accurately how we were all related—Claire, Ainsley, and I being former schoolmates, Ainsley now marrying her best friend's father.

But then the writer exaggerated, writing in a very tabloid-like fashion. She detailed Todd's out of control partying and Claire being banned from Bergdorf Goodman but both still getting into good colleges, quite clearly inferring the D'Angelo's wealth was both to blame and to thank.

And there was a paragraph all about Ned D'Angelo being investigated by the government for his financial arrangements. She said there, again, about his skill as a tax avoider. What exactly was she trying to say?

Even though the article was about the murder, there was only a small paragraph about Joey and his demise. Felicity knew he was a private investigator, but a simple internet search would tell her that. Just as bad, her linking his death to me and the others was tenuous at best: we were all from New York and had arrived within days of each other.

Auntie Akamai stomped back in with a cup of coffee and a roll in one hand, her phone glued to her ear with the other. "An investigative piece?" She rolled her eyes, banged the cup and food down on the table, and stormed out again. "It's trash!" The last thing I heard after my door banged shut was a threat about discussing this with his mother at their next Mahjong club get together.

I wouldn't want to hear that conversation. Or the one between the Mahjong Mother and her son.

I reread the article and nibbled absentmindedly at the buttery roll, still warm from the oven. I stopped again on the paragraph about the D'Angelo's troubles. I'm not sure what was snagging my attention. Probably the gossipy feel about people I knew. But were those things true? It certainly wasn't true that I was arrested for murder, so I couldn't be sure the other assertations weren't fictional as well.

I folded the paper and stuck it under my arm, carrying the cup and remnants of the roll with me to Auntie Akamai's kitchen. She was still on the phone or likely talking to her Mahjong friend now. I pantomimed "computer" to her, and she nodded, pointing at the living room, but pushed another roll into my hand before I left.

Paulie was in the living room, and as soon as I sat down, he began to edge closer to me, eyeballing the roll in my hand.

"No," I told him. "I don't know if it's okay for you to eat."

He squawked, ruffled his feathers, and began to click his beak, something he didn't stop doing the entire time I was there.

I set the laptop on my knees and opened the browser. I spent the next hour reading articles about Todd and Claire. It sounded like they had had some troubles for sure. The snippet in the gossip section about Claire being escorted out of the department store said there had been "some confusion about payment." The pictures of Todd were much more straightforward. No doubt the boy liked to party.

I looked for them on social media and was very surprised to not find any accounts on any of the common social media sites. Ainsley, on the other hand, was plastered all over various sites, including TikTok. She had a decent number of followers too. I wondered if those would magically disappear once she was married to a society man, especially because her TikToks mainly consisted of her doing little dances in clothes that were too small.

I almost gave up looking for anything about Ned and his financial issues, and then I found one tiny article referring to the IRS auditing his company. I will admit I got a C in Economics 101 and frankly had no idea about half the words in the article. By this point my coffee was gone, and my back was getting stiff.

Auntie Akamai read my mind and was holding the steaming coffee carafe in her hand when I walked into the kitchen. I held my cup out, and she filled it.

She appeared to be much calmer now. "Find anything interesting?"

"That article is hardly an investigative piece. Everything could be found via an internet search, and it's not like she solved the murder." I blew across the surface of my coffee to cool it.

Auntie Akamai rolled her eyes. "She's a hack. And what about your computer time? Learn anything?"

I frowned. "Just confirmed some of the things she said about the D'Angelos."

She raised her eyebrows and made a "go on" motion with her hand.

"Todd is quite the partier, and it looks like Claire got caught shoplifting, but it was swept under the rug. And Ned, his company was audited by the IRS." I took a long sip of my coffee but couldn't swallow because Auntie Akamai shocked me by breaking into laughter.

"I can't believe I didn't see it!" She smacked herself in the forehead, then pointed to a copy of the list of codes she had hung on her refrigerator. "*TE*!"

I shook my head and raised my shoulders. "What?"

"*TE*!" She pointed at the list. "Tax evasion! That's one big reason to be audited by the IRS, if there are suspicions."

I leaned closer to read the code following Ned's initials. *ND-TE1/2M,0/125K,0* "Ned D'Angelo, tax evasion." I nodded. "That makes sense. But what does the 'one' following it mean?"

She pursed her lips. "I have no idea yet. My eyes tend to read all numbers as money, but the letters are confusing. I've figured various math equations using roman numerals, the minus sign, the back slashes, but nothing makes sense unless perhaps the one-slash-two means one half."

I leaned over and squinted at the paper. "So the *M*… One half million?"

"I think so. That would line up with the *K* being for thousands. But a half million doesn't seem like a big enough sum to evade taxes for." She sighed. "We'll figure it out."

I studied the paper a moment longer, sipping my coffee again. "So we need to figure out what the letter part of the codes mean, and what they mean in relation to the dollar amounts."

She held up a finger. "*If* that's what they are. I don't want to commit fully to a theory and become blind to other options."

This was a smart woman. "Well, I guess we should take a break for the time being. I need to shower."

She smiled her wide, beautiful smile and winked. "Yes,

you have another date with my nephew. He asked me to let you know he'd be here at two o'clock. The diving excursion today was a sunrise dive."

I blew out a breath. "Oh good. I was worried I offended him last night and he didn't want to go."

Her eyes twinkled. "Oh, if he was being mopey it's only because he likes you so much."

"Really?"

"Oh yes. He is quite taken with you." She raised a hand and patted my cheek.

I could feel the color rising in my cheeks. "Oh." I ducked my head and averted my eyes while I gulped down the last of my coffee…and then choked on it and had a coughing fit.

Auntie Akamai banged me on the back, chuckling.

"I like him too," I gasped, my eyes streaming. I gave her a weak smile, put my empty mug in the sink, and retreated to my furnished lanai.

* * *

After my shower, I stood in front of my closet in my towel, debating what to wear. Maybe my little skirt with a nicer blouse, not a ratty T-shirt this time? He had seen the skirt before at the bar, but it was my understanding guys usually didn't remember details like that.

I flipped through the things in my closet and decided I wanted to wear a top I had left in the suitcase. And the sandals I wore on the plane were in there too. I went to the bed and pulled it out, unzipped, and opened it.

It was empty.

I gasped and felt around just in case my eyes were deceiving me. There was something there but not a single piece of clothing.

All of my expensive clothes had been stolen, and a USB drive was left in their place.

CHAPTER SIXTEEN

———

"Auntie Akamai!" I rushed into the house, startling her and Paulie both.

"Goodness, girl, what?!" Auntie Akamai stroked Paulie's ruffled feathers. "It's okay, pretty bird."

Paulie clicked his beak and glared at me.

I bit back tears (*stupid tears!*) and told her how my suitcase was empty.

She stood abruptly. "Was there anything valuable? Oh, golly, I should have had you bring valuables into the house." She clamped her hand to her forehead. "Why didn't I think about that?"

"It's not your fault." I reached out a hand and patted her arm. "It's usually not a problem, right?"

"Oh," she sighed. "But I heard from my friend the other day—the one who was here in the yard, you remember?"

I nodded, and she continued.

"She works at the resort and was telling me there has been a rash of robberies. Or is it burglaries?" She tapped her lip, looking at the ceiling. "Burglaries. Anyway, there have been several at the resort."

"But that was at the resort. Why would you worry about your property out here?" I tried to remember if I had locked the door behind me when I'd left. All I had to do was push the button on the inside. I had thought it funny since anyone really wanting to get in could just cut the wall of screen and enter that way.

I realized Auntie Akamai must have said something, as she was staring at me. "I'm sorry, what?"

"Was there anything valuable?"

I pursed my lips. "Depends what you see as valuable I guess. Just clothes, but my favorite sandals. I had put my jewelry in the pantry, in a pot. It was still there."

Auntie Akamai's eyebrows drew together. "Clothes? Someone stole clothes? Were they expensive articles?"

I nodded. "Most, yes."

She crossed her arms, sizing me up. "Not things I would have known were expensive."

My eyes widened. "No, no. I'm not accusing you!"

She chuckled. "I know you're not, girlie. I'm saying there aren't many people around here who know expensive clothes when they see them. Maybe the girls at the boutiques, but I'm going to take a wild guess and say it wasn't a local. But it *was* someone who knew a rich girl was living in my lanai."

Who knew I was here? Samantha and her friends, but they were locals. Dex, the detective, and anyone Auntie Akamai told, probably all locals as well.

Ainsley. She and Ned brought me by here before the disastrous sailing trip.

Before I could voice my thought, Auntie Akamai slapped the kitchen counter with a hand. "The article told everyone you were here! Oh, when I get my hands on her…"

I had forgotten about that for a wonderful few moments. *The Heiress in the Shack.* I frowned. "I'm not an heiress, by the way. I mean, I guess I am, but I don't think like that about my parents' mortality." I pointed at the paper on the counter. "It doesn't give a thief much time though. The story came out this morning, and I was only in the house with you a few hours. I don't think someone read the article then came over here."

Auntie Akamai made a stink face, like she was upset she couldn't blame it on Felicity Chase's article. "Well, unless it was Felicity herself, but I've never known her to be a criminal. Sneaky and low, but not criminal." She snorted. "Except for trespassing." She took a step toward the phone attached to the kitchen wall. "We should call the police."

"Well, wait." I hesitated, then pulled the thumb drive from the pocket of the shorts I had thrown on in my haste. "There is this, too."

Auntie Akamai squinted. "What? A computer thing?"

"It's a memory stick, or thumb drive. They hold files and plug into the USB port of a computer. But it's not mine. Why would I carry one without having a computer with me?" I held it out to her. "All the clothes were gone, but this was left in their place."

Auntie Akamai pulled a napkin from the holder on the counter and gently took it from me, using the napkin. Why hadn't I thought of that? She held it up to her eye. "No markings." She looked up at me. "Shall we take a look? It might shed some light on who took your stuff, though it may have been a deliberate act, not a mistake."

"*Son of a gun!*" Paulie flapped his wings. "*You stinking rat!*"

Auntie Akamai pursed her lips and swung her head to look at the clock over the stove. "Dex must be here."

"Oh! I need to change!"

Auntie Akamai looked me up and down. "You look fine."

"But…"

"It's Hawaii, girlie. You're fine."

"*Rat fink!*" Paulie took off and flew out the doorway to the living room, and I could hear Dex talking to him.

I took a deep breath and gestured at the thumb drive. "Why don't we look at this when I get back," I whispered.

She nodded and slipped it into a counter drawer right as Dex walked in.

"Hi." He smiled at me. "You look nice."

I blushed and glanced down at my clothes. "Thanks."

"Are you ready?" His smile extended to his eyes and made me feel warm.

Giving Auntie Akamai a meaningful look, shooting my eyes at the drawer which held the drive, I waved to her as I followed him out.

* * *

Walking down the pier next to Dex, I listened to him as he pointed out various places where activities were held. Apparently the resort hosted hula lessons, luaus, weddings…

I stopped short. *Is this where Ainsley's wedding will be held?*

"Is there a program of events?" I looked around for a billboard.

"I think at the resort. Why?" Dex stared down at me.

I shrugged. "You know. In case I want to do any of those things."

His eyebrows jetted up. Then realization dawned in his eyes. "Oh, you want to know about the wedding of your friends."

"Not friends," I said a little too heatedly. I shook my head and continued more gently. "I'd say acquaintances maybe. Associates? People I used to know?" I reached out and gently squeezed his hand to soften my harsh tone.

"Well, isn't that them, walking onto the pier over there?" He pointed behind me.

I spun, saw the group, then pulled Dex with me as I ran for cover. A photo booth. *How convenient!* I pulled the curtain closed.

Dex chuckled as we were pressed together in the booth. "Well, okay. You could've asked." He let go of my hand to dig into his pocket for his wallet.

Well, this wasn't what I was going for, but it would work. Two birds with one stone?

And wow did he smell good!

We sat on the little bench, squashed together, and he leaned forward to feed bills into the hungry money slot. I watched as he bought two sessions.

He leaned back. "Can I put my arm around you?"

I smiled up at him. "Yes. Thank you for asking."

He slipped his arm around, and we smiled at the square screen in front of us. On the screen, numbers counted down to one, and there was a flash. The picture appeared on the screen.

It was nice but a bit *American Gothic*, the painting with the farmer couple who look less than absolutely thrilled with life.

"That's a bit boring. Maybe I should do this—" Right as the number one flashed up, Dex poked me in the side, making me shriek.

Which made for a more interesting picture, for sure.

The third was us laughing, him leaning back in self-defense with his hands raised.

Then I heard familiar voices outside. I froze, and Dex

followed suit.

"At least the idiot can't drive here," a voice said.

"Thank goodness. Last thing Ned needs is another DUI to cover up."

I tipped my head, thinking. Ned had a DUI?

Picture four was of us gawking at the curtain.

Those voices faded, and others got into the audible range.

"I don't understand why we have to have a meeting," the voice whined.

"I think that was Claire." I leaned close to whisper to Dex.

"We have to get our stories straight." *Heather?*

Picture five was me leaning in toward him, my face inches from his as I whispered that the speaker was Heather, Claire's mother.

Picture six was his hand coming to my cheek, us staring into each other's eyes, our lips within inches of each other.

Picture seven…both of us screaming and jumping when a loud, boisterous male voice banged on the side of the photo booth, shaking it, and threatening to tip it over.

Picture eight was me holding Dex back from leaping out of the booth.

Once I calmed him, I peeked out of the curtain and watched Todd as he staggered after the rest of his family. He had a strip of photos in his hand.

I looked at the slot on the outside of the photo booth and saw that it was empty, then looked back and watched as Todd gave them a cursory glance and threw them off the pier.

I slumped back down on the bench inside the booth. They may not have been the best photos, but they were of us. Ours.

"What?" Dex looked down at me.

"Todd grabbed our photos and threw them away."

"What?!" He half rose, then sat again. "Both strips?"

"Oh. I don't know. Two copies come out?"

"Yeah. One for you and one for me." Dex grinned.

"Oh, duh. That makes sense." I smiled sheepishly.

"Never done one of these before?" Dex asked.

"Not since like high school." I gestured at the screen. "In the days before digital."

Dex laughed as he stood and popped his head out between the curtains. He stretched his top half out for a moment, then pulled himself back in. He brandished a strip of photos like a sword. "Now we have to fight over who gets them." He looked at the photos in the strip. "Or cut it in half."

"The long way or the short way?" I laughed and made a dumb face as I took them. I folded the pictures carefully in half along the white picture border and slipped them into my back pocket. "Let's go see if we can find the other set."

We stood, and then I giggled nervously. Why was it we seemed closer together when standing?

We poked our heads out of the curtain, his above mine, probably looking very comical. I snickered again and raised my head to nudge his chin, then turned and looked right. The group was fifty feet or so away, clustered in a knot.

I slipped out and to the left, keeping the photo booth between me and the other New Yorkers. Dex followed, and when I leaned to peer around the corner, his hands went to my waist as he leaned out too. It was totally innocent—I held on to him on the motorcycle this same way, after all—but it felt so personal. I tried not to react. And then he leaned down and spoke close to my ear, making my hairs tickle me.

"Let's go to the pylon next."

I nodded, then hurried forward, trying to keep the large wooden post between our prey and me. Once I arrived, I looked down into the water.

Dex arrived after me and looked down too. "There they are." He pointed. "What a jerk."

Raised voices, still too far to be understood, caught our attention again.

"The shaved ice cart next?" I asked.

Dex nodded, so I started off, keeping a bicycle-pulled cart in the line of sight between us and the family cluster. Very conveniently, it had a large umbrella tipped at an angle.

We were maybe twenty feet away now, but still couldn't understand them. I looked at Dex.

"We could try casually walking by?" He shrugged.

I pursed my lips. "I don't want them to see me."

"But this is fun." Dex had a mischievous glint in his eye. "And aren't you curious what the 'family meeting' is about, what story they have to get straight?"

"It could be a wedding rehearsal. There could be things to get worked out?" But right as I said that, Susan's voice raised above the others, and Ned shouted back.

"What was that?" Dex sucked in a breath. "Did he say murder?!"

It's what I heard too, and when I peeked around the umbrella, saw Claire and Todd's mother, Heather, glancing around and shushing them. Other passersby had taken notice of the heated argument. The group continued arguing, but much more quietly.

"Well, I think that is that." I turned my body halfway. "We aren't going to hear now and can't get any closer."

"Sure we can." Dex craned his head for our next hiding spot.

The shaved ice cart guy poked his head around the umbrella. "You guys want shaved ice, or you just gonna keep hiding behind my umbrella?"

Laughing, Dex waved off the guy. "We'll come back later."

We waited for a group of tourists to approach, then slid in beside them. After we passed the family group, now clustered between the pier railing and a booth selling hats, we separated from the tourists and hid alongside the booth. Backs against it, I did a quick peek around at the D'Angelo-Rickenbacker-Jameson family.

"He was here for Katherine, you know," said Claire rather loudly.

"Right, so whoever did this didn't need to have done it!" Ainsley pointed at Heather. "The man wasn't even here about us."

Heather's face turned dark red, and she looked like she could spit nails. "Well, maybe if some people could keep their hands off…"

"Heather, chill out," slurred her son. "Leave the skank alone."

"Hey son, don't call Ainsley a skank." Ned straightened and glared at his son.

Todd turned toward the booth—and me—and I hid back around the side. He lumbered by, muttering, "She was *my* skank."

"Aw, now that's sweet," whispered Dex.

I hit his arm, and in return, he handed me a huge, floppy straw hat with a blue and white Hawaiian print ribbon around it. I took it before he pulled me around to the front of the booth just as the family passed where we had been. I put on my hat, and laughed when I saw his new hat—a winter knit hat with braids coming off the side flaps and a large poof on top.

Armed with our disguises, we meshed ourselves into a group of people watching a juggler. I ended up right behind Claire and her twin, Todd. Dex stood by my right side.

"You need to stop it with the drinking," she hissed. "You look like a fool, and you know you can't control your dumb mouth when you're sloshed! You're gonna say stuff you shouldn't!"

"Like what. You don't think anyone will notice you have two suitcases instead of one when we get on the plane to get away from this dump?" He laughed, then wiped his nose on the back of his hand.

"Claire! Todd!" An arm came between Dex and me and grabbed at Claire's shirt. I turned away to the left just in time to shield my face from their mother, Heather, as she pushed her way between us. "Come on, you two. Your new mommy is getting whiney about the sun and your father wants to feed her." She yanked Claire backward, and Claire in turn pulled Todd.

I peeked back over my shoulder and saw that Dex had turned completely to the right and was standing stiff and tall like a statue. I giggled. "They're gone."

He turned and looked down at me, his smile making me feel warm.

We snuck out of the crowd and looked around for the family group, but they were way off in the distance now, walking back toward the resort.

After going back to get the promised shaved ice, we meandered toward the end of the pier to a bench. We sat and talked until the sun was low in the sky. Little butterflies flapped around in my belly when Dex casually reached over and took my hand. We stayed watching the sky turn violent shades of pink and orange, even after the sun sank below the sparkling waves.

CHAPTER SEVENTEEN

———

After a rather chaste peck on the cheek and a hug, I headed around the edge of the house toward my lanai.

"Psst," whispered Auntie Akamai from her own screened in porch at the back of her house. It startled me so much that I tripped on one of the Banyan tree roots.

"*Sssssss*," repeated Paulie. Not a bad attempt.

I smiled and headed over to her.

"You alone?" She craned her neck like I was hiding Dex behind me. Like I could hide an over six-something foot muscle-bound man behind me. I was five-five.

"Of course I am." I tried to sound offended, but it sounded stuck up instead. "It was our second date!"

I could hear her soft laughter as I climbed the steps. "Did you have a nice time?"

I smiled. "Yes. We got these pictures done. Let me show you." I held them out and narrated what was happening in each. (Except for the one where it looked like we were about to kiss. I glossed quickly over that one.) She listened, enthralled, as I outlined our sneaky mission before we gave up and had shaved ice.

She smiled politely. "Sounds like you had fun." Without waiting for a response, she grabbed my arm and pulled me to the kitchen. "Come on. Come see what I was doing. Not quite as fun but just as interesting!"

She dragged me to her laptop on the dinette table. "I'm sorry, but I couldn't wait for you to see what was on the memory stick."

"It's okay. What's there?" I sat down at the table and leaned toward the computer eagerly. "I had a hard time not thinking about it the whole time." *Not quite the truth…*

"Well," said Auntie Akamai, clearly enjoying the upper hand, "let's just say we should probably *not* call the police. Yet."

I stared at her. "What? Why?"

"This," she said, holding up the thumb drive, "belongs to Joey Morton." She let her dramatic statement sink in, then added, "I think."

I couldn't help but laugh. "Why do you think that?"

"Because there are folders labeled with the same initials as the list." She sat back, arms crossed, looking supremely satisfied.

"Seriously?" I stared.

She nodded. "Yes. But that's where the excitement ends. I have no idea what the contents of the folders mean."

I tipped my head. "What are they?"

"Documents. Copies of newspaper articles. Emails." She shrugged. "We'll need to really study them to understand. I started a list of contents of each file." She gestured to a notepad next to the computer.

"Maybe we should turn it in to the detective?" I scratched at a colored flake on the Formica tabletop.

"Kiki"—Auntie Akamai leaned toward me—"how are you going to explain having this?"

I hadn't thought that far ahead. "I know. But it does mean," I pointed out, "it's highly likely the thief who left it is also involved with the murder."

She nodded. "Yes, that's what I'm saying, minus the theft part. What if the detective thinks you made it up about your clothes being stolen? That you *just happened* to find this in your suitcase? In your lanai?"

I could easily picture the detective's skeptical look. "And my fingerprints are on it." I dropped my head into my hands.

"Oh, I've cleaned it, and we will clean it each time we finish looking at it." She lowered herself onto a chair with a small groan. "Let me show you what I've found."

She put the drive into the USB port, and while it was opening up, she pointed to the notepad. "I started with *HD*, Heather D'Angelo. Hers I think I have figured out." She opened the folder and showed me a newspaper article that talked about a college cheating scandal. No names were mentioned, but it did mention one of the cases had two students in the same family having their entrance exams and high school grades fudged. Auntie Akamai pointed, running her finger along the screen as she read a digitally highlighted section.

"Then this." It was another newspaper article about the scandal, a few weeks later. The same newspaper and same article author, the same highlighted paragraph about the suspects almost verbatim. *Almost* because the line about the two related students was gone.

"Maybe the author just forgot?" I ventured.

"Or maybe someone paid for the case to go away."

I tapped my lip. "And with it being in *HD*'s file, we think this means Heather was the one cheating to get her kids into college. And Heather made it disappear, but Joey found out."

Auntie Akamai nodded and pointed at another file. "This is a deposition with the names of all the accused. No Heather D'Angelo."

I looked toward the refrigerator and read the code posted there. "*HD-CC50K,com*. Heather D'Angelo, college cheating."

"Yes!" Auntie Akamai clapped her hands. "That was what I was thinking too!"

"Did she pay fifty thousand to get them in school, then?" I toggled back over to the file folder. "Is there an article that says how much the cheaters were fined?"

There was not another file, so I pulled up the internet browser and typed in "college cheating scandal results." Auntie Akamai came behind me and read over my shoulder as I scanned, reading parts out loud about the people who were convicted. "They got jail time! And fines…this one over a million and this one two hundred thousand. That's way more." I sat back, shaking my head. "It doesn't add up. If she cheated to get both Todd and Claire into college, her fine would probably be more than a million since it was two individual sets of records."

Auntie Akamai sunk back into her chair, nodding, a frown on her face. "A good question as well is why Joey Morton—or whoever's drive this is—had a list in the first place."

"If I didn't already know he came here to find me, it would really look like he followed them here." I drummed my fingers on the table. "We need to find out why he had that list."

Auntie Akamai sighed and rubbed her eyes. She wasn't used to staring at a computer screen.

I leaned forward and patted her hand. "Why don't you get some sleep. You did good investigative work."

She nodded, smiling. "Thank you." She grasped my hand back, hers warm and soft. "We need to look at the rest of these though, figure out their codes before we turn over the drive."

I nodded. "We will. And I'll copy the files to the computer hard drive. But I think our next move is to talk to Heather D'Angelo. See if we can get her alone, and maybe without any of the others she'll give us information to make this clearer."

* * *

I was a little nervous about sleeping out in my burgled lanai, so I "accidentally" fell asleep on the couch with the computer next to me. I mean, I did do more research of Joey's USB drive, annotating documents on Auntie Akamai's list as I went. I skipped around in order to keep my interest. And when I was finally tired enough, I cuddled around a throw pillow and went to sleep.

I was woken by whispering. Auntie Akamai and Dex were in the kitchen packing up the lunches she'd made for today's dive excursion. I couldn't decipher any of their words and, since I was lying on my side with my back to the room, continued to "sleep" until Dex left. I didn't want him to see me all unbrushed and morning breathy!

Shortly after he left, Auntie Akamai tiptoed in and set a cup of coffee on the table behind me. "He's gone now, girlie. You can stop pretending to be asleep."

I couldn't help but smile. "Good morning." I rolled over and pulled myself to a sit. I pushed off a blanket some blanket fairy had put over me when I was asleep.

Auntie Akamai lowered herself into her chair with a sigh. She reached and picked up the notebook and looked over my notes. "So you think Todd was in trouble for drunk driving. Which makes sense with the *DD*."

"Yeah." I stretched my arms above my head and leaned from side to side. "I didn't think it was going to be Dunkin' Donuts."

"What? He can't like donuts?" Auntie Akamai chuckled.

I laughed. "I bet none of the D'Angelo group touches the things."

Auntie Akamai studied me. "You're different from them."

"I hope so!" I laughed. "When I left for college, it was eye-opening. I insisted on staying in a dorm with the peasants, as my father joked. I didn't want to pledge in my mother's sorority, much to her chagrin." I picked up my coffee and took a long draft. "I wanted to be as far away from New York as I could, and Seattle is definitely not the East Coast. Couldn't be more different. Plus they have a good program for Marine Biology at the University of Washington. They have research facilities in the San Juans…" I trailed off when Auntie Akamai sputtered and started choking on her coffee. "Are you okay?"

Auntie Akamai nodded, coughing and wiping at her eyes. She looked down at her dress and wiped at it, though if there was spilled coffee it was impossible to see in the crazy print. "You went to University of Washington?"

I nodded. "Yes. Why?"

"Did Dex not tell you where he went?"

I shook my head but thought back to our conversation about college. "He didn't even tell me he went to college. He seemed impressed I had."

She nodded. "Probably because he couldn't think of how to mention it without talking about his ex-girlfriend. Well, ex-fiancée."

My stomach filled with rocks. "He never mentioned a fiancée."

She waved a hand. "Ex-fiancée. She even came to Kauai to work at the shop." She stretched over and patted my knee. "It was a year ago."

"Is that the person who left that I was supposed to be replacing?" I set my coffee down.

"Well, I suppose so." She eyed me. "Everyone has a history, you know." She waved a hand at the computer. "Sort of like these folks. They have things in their history that Joey dug up. But just because they did things in the past doesn't mean they do them now."

My gaze followed her wave to the computer. "Except some do. Look at Todd. He's clearly still having an issue with drinking." I paused, staring into space and thinking about what Dex and I had overheard in the photo booth. *At least the idiot can't drive here...last thing Ned needs is another DUI to cover up.*

"Earth to Kiki?" Auntie Akamai said. "What's going on in there?"

I looked up at her. "The codes. I've been going over them." I ran to the kitchen and pulled the sheet off the refrigerator, waving it in the air as I returned to the couch.

> *ND-TE1/2M,0/I25K,0*
> *CD-CC10K,com/S&T75K,0*
> *TD-DD,R,R?25K(10K)*
> *HD-CC50K,com*
> *SJ-F500K/I25K,com*
> *AR-D10K,com*

I pointed at the "*TD*" line. "The evidence on the memory stick points to Todd having been caught for drunk driving, right?"

"Or drunk and disorderly." Aunt Akamai looked pleased. "I just thought of that. It's *DD* as well."

"Right, yes. But like his mother, Heather, the charges seemed to have disappeared, at least from the papers. And one of them said yesterday something about Ned covering up a DUI." I thrusted out a hand and pointed at the computer. "Claire has been caught stealing, but the paparazzi seemed to have dropped that story as well. Joey figured this out. He realized Ned was using his money to cover up his children's and wife's misdeeds."

I looked at her, urging her to see the link I saw. Or at least thought I saw.

"And Joey wanted a piece of the pie." She nodded all her chins enthusiastically. "The *K*s are money amounts!"

We said it in stereo. "*Blackmail.*"

CHAPTER EIGHTEEN

After I cleaned up, we headed to the resort to find and talk to Heather D'Angelo. Auntie Akamai whispered to a girl behind the counter who nodded, tapped at the computer for a moment, and then picked up her phone. After a short conversation, she hung up and relayed whatever she learned to Auntie Akamai.

Auntie Akamai returned to me with a smile. "She's in the spa."

Auntie Akamai led the way. I hadn't been there, and though I might have wanted to stay in a nice hotel, it didn't mean I needed to use my parents' money for frivolous purposes. (Other than diving, of course.)

We settled into big soft chairs in the waiting room and listened to the soft, relaxing music. It smelled like eucalyptus, and there were fake, battery-operated candles everywhere. I was about to nod off when I heard a door open and close down the hall. A few moments later a woman in a resort uniform polo shirt appeared. She nodded at us but didn't stop or ask us what we needed.

Several minutes later, Heather appeared. She had a beatific smile on her glowing face and looked a bit drowsy. I quickly lifted the magazine I was reading up to cover my face.

"Okay," whispered Auntie Akamai, "let's go."

I hopped up and followed her out. She went outside and settled herself into a chair at a table on the patio looking out over the water.

"*Aloha*. May we join you?" Auntie Akamai asked.

"What? Who are you?" Heather asked. Then her eyes fell on me. "Oh, it's you."

Without waiting for Heather to say it was okay, Auntie

Akamai squeezed herself into a chair and settled in. Heather was watching her with a curled lip, like she smelled something bad.

What a snob.

"What do you want?" Heather gave me a glare.

"Did you break the rules to get the twins into college?" I figured why beat around the bush.

Her eyes narrowed further, almost to slits. "Where did you hear that?"

"A friend," said Auntie Akamai.

Heather gave her a glance then turned her body toward me, making it clear she didn't consider Auntie Akamai worth talking to. "I bet. Susan, probably?"

Aunt Akamai made a noncommittal noise, which only served to incense Heather. She launched into a diatribe about Ainsley's mother. Nothing she said piqued my interest until she said Susan had her secrets too.

"And what is Susan hiding?" I interrupted her, which turned out to be a dumb move. I should have let her rail on about her nemesis because now she turned her sights on me.

"What about you and your secrets, Katherine? What exactly are you hiding?" She sneered at me, then lifted an arm at a passing waiter. "Tequila Sunrise. Top shelf, none of the garbage, and don't be skimpy with it." When the waiter, a young Hawaiian native with hair that fell stylishly across his forehead, had the audacity to look at Auntie Akamai and me, she exploded at him. "*Those* people get *nothing*!" The waiter looked scared and scurried away.

"Little early for booze, isn't it, Mrs. D'Angelo?" I smiled saccharine sweet. "Or is this where Todd gets his day drinking habits?"

She raised her pencil-thin brows at me. "So were your parents abusing you? How long had it gone on? Does Daddy love his little girl a little too much?"

"What?!" I bolted up and out of my chair. "No! Why would you say that!?"

Her shark-like smile returned. "Why else would you run away from home?"

I rolled my eyes and sat down. "I did not run away from home. For goodness' sake, I'm almost twenty-three and have a college degree. Most of my classmates have actual jobs at this point." I gave a short laugh. "Of course, I'm not referring to *your* children."

She glared at me. "Of course not. They don't need to debase themselves."

Auntie Akamai snorted. "Debase themselves by working like mature adults? They did that themselves in other ways on their own, didn't they?"

Heather shifted her entire body to look at Auntie Akamai. "And who exactly are you again?"

Auntie Akamai said some words in a different language, causing Heather to stare.

"Mrs. D'Angelo, I have a question." I leaned forward to catch her attention back. "The first day we saw each other, on the boat. You laughed when I asked you not to tell my parents you saw me here. If you thought they were abusive, why would you laugh?"

Heather threw back her head and laughed like a hyena. The waiter had the misfortune of approaching at that moment. Heather snatched the offered drink from him like it was her checkbook, without the slightest hint of gratitude. "Girl," she said, turning on me, "I was laughing because I knew they were going to know anyway. I knew Joey was here to find you. The gig was up. I never thought you'd kill him over it."

Before I could respond Auntie Akamai put her hand up. "Jig."

"Excuse me? Did you speak?" Heather practically snarled.

"It's the jig is up, not the gig is up," Auntie Akamai said quietly.

"I. Don't. Care," Heather snapped before turning her sights back on me. "Did you not wonder where your parents would have come across someone as scummy as Joey Morton?"

Actually, yes. I raised my shoulders.

Heather leaned toward me, her tequila-laced breath reaching me. "I'm the one who introduced them to Joey." She leaned back, satisfied by the shocked look I must've had on my face. "Well, passed on his number, I mean. I didn't introduce them in person." She gave a little shiver, like the thought was disturbing.

"So you're admitting you knew him before coming here." I put my arms on the table with my hands on top of each other.

She leaned forward again. "Duh."

"So how did you meet him? I mean, I heard he was the one you hired to spy on Ned. Where did you meet him to use his services then?" I waited with bated breath for this answer.

She faltered, as I figured she would. "He, um, approached me a year or two ago with a business proposal."

Auntie Akamai snorted and looked at me. "Is that how rich people refer to being blackmailed?"

Heather turned beet red, and I wasn't sure if she was embarrassed or about to blow her top.

"You're looking a little sunburnt, Mrs. D'Angelo." I motioned my hand around my own face.

"Then I had better go to the shade." Heather gritted her teeth but still managed to enunciate. "And stop calling me Mrs. D'Angelo."

As she stood, I reached out a hand. "What am I supposed to call you then?"

"You? Nothing. You're *nothing*, so don't address me as anything ever again."

And with that she stormed away, leaving her drained glass behind.

The waiter appeared the second she was gone and picked up her glass. Auntie Akamai dug into one of her pockets and pulled out a few bills to hand him.

"Oh, thanks. None of her group ever tip." He blushed, then leaned over, causing his hair to flop over one eye, and whispered. "Please don't tell anyone I said that."

"Has her group been out here together?" I had seen them as a group myself, but the way they were fighting, my thoughts were it wouldn't be a common occurrence.

"Oh yeah. A couple times." He pushed his fop of hair back into place.

"Really? Which ones? Her and who else?" I asked, and Auntie Akamai nodded encouragingly.

"Um, well, there's a younger lady and a young man.

They seem to be her kids?" He looked up into the blue sky. "Then an older man, another young lady—she hangs all over the man—and another older lady. She grabbed my bum once." He blushed scarlet.

"I'm sorry they treat you that way." Auntie Akamai dug into her pocket again and pulled out more bills and set them on the table.

"Can you remember anything else about them? How did they behave, other than rudely?" I felt terrible I came from the same background as these people. My mother might be a cold shrew to me, but she was never rude to service staff. She always said you need to be polite to people who handle your food.

"Oh," the young man began, his eyes on the money. "They were plenty rude to each other too. Bickered the whole time. Pretty drunk and belligerent. They were really bothering other parties, but my manager didn't want to upset them further." He looked up. "The one time they got quiet and I came by to see if they needed anything, that lady yelled at me. Said to stop eavesdropping or she'd get me fired."

"Were you eavesdropping?" Auntie Akamai looked surprised.

"No, of course not. I did hear things, but not on purpose, you know?" The waiter was beginning to look scared again.

"It's okay, we understand. We would never do anything to get you fired." Auntie Akamai spoke gently, like she was calming a horse. She slid the money toward him and gestured for him to take it. "I'm assuming they didn't tip you that night either. This is to make up for it."

"Thank you, ma'am." He took the money, glancing around, and stuck it into his pocket. He hesitated a moment, jiggling his leg. "I did hear something before the lady yelled at me about eavesdropping. It doesn't make a lot of sense, but maybe it will to you?"

Auntie Akamai murmured and nodded.

"I heard one of them say 'we have to blame tiki'. I thought they might be talking about the Lava Pot, like maybe reporting them for letting the young guy drink so much. I'd hate to see Casey or his staff get in trouble."

I leaned forward. "Tiki? Could they have said *Kiki*?"

The boy thought for a moment, then nodded. "Yeah, they might have said that."

CHAPTER NINETEEN

———

Auntie Akamai didn't try to stop me or my tirade. She simply followed me as I stalked out of the resort, my words pouring forth in a tsunami.

Of course they were going to blame it on me. Blame it on the one outside the dysfunctional family group. Blame it on the one inadvertently and tenuously connected to the murdered man.

When I stopped to let a car pass, I heard Auntie Akamai's breathing behind me. The poor woman was going to pass out trying to keep up with me. I turned and held out a hand to her shoulder.

"I'm sorry. I'm ranting." I took a deep breath to steady myself.

"It's okay. I get it." She put her hands on her hips and panted. "It has occurred to me that you are also here without protection of your own family, or ability to get and pay for a lawyer."

I sighed and looked at the sky. "I hadn't even thought about it. But yeah."

"Do you think Joey had contacted your parents?"

I thought about it for a moment. "Probably. But there was no sign in my emails. They have emailed but not recently, and nothing saying they know where I am."

She narrowed her eyes at me. "And did you answer their emails?"

"Yes, ma'am." I mock saluted her. "Short and vague, but yes."

She shook her head slowly. "It makes me sad for you that you and your mother are not closer. My daughter, we are tight." She placed her palms together to show how close they were.

"*Ohana*, right?" I smiled weakly, remembering one of the few Hawaiian words I knew from a movie.

"Yes, girlie. *Ohana*. Family you are born to—or family you choose." She reached out and grasped one of my hands in hers.

I squeezed her hand back, gratitude for having met this woman flowing through me. "What was it you said to Heather? In Hawaiian, I assume?"

She smiled. "She asked me who I was. I said *Ku'ia kahele aka na'au ha'aha'a*, which means *A humble person walks carefully so as not to hurt others*."

"That's beautiful. It's a saying?"

She nodded. "I figured it was as good an answer as anything else." She dropped my hand and gestured. "So where are you headed?"

I shrugged. "Nowhere really, just stomping around."

We laughed, and then Auntie Akamai spotted something—or someone—over my shoulder, and her smile faded. I turned.

It was Detective Ray.

"Ladies." He sauntered over like he had not a care in the world. "I was about to head out to your house, Auntie. I have some more questions for Miss Barrington."

"Let me guess, Ray. Some more 'sources' have fed you information about her?" Auntie Akamai crossed her arms and straightened to her full height. She was a formidable-looking woman when she wanted to be.

"I received an anonymous call about searching your…apartment."

"Oh, let me guess." I rolled my eyes. "The caller indicated something belonging to Mr. Morton would be found there."

Detective Ray flicked his eyes between us.

"Well, I can save you some time." Auntie Akamai reached into one of her miraculous pockets and pulled out the USB drive. "They are probably referring to this."

Detective Ray looked at it. "I think I need more of an explanation."

"I was robbed. Everything in my suitcase was taken, and this was there instead." I pointed at Auntie Akamai's outstretched hand.

"Robbed?" Detective Ray frowned.

"She means burgled. Someone came when she was gone and took all her items." Auntie Akamai flapped her other hand like it was no consequence.

I turned to her. "You said that before. What's the difference?"

"Robbery is of a person, like being mugged. Burglary is of a place." Detective Ray explained to me. "Now, did you report the theft?"

I laughed. "No." I gestured at the USB drive again. "Precisely because of what you will think when you see what this is."

"Well, what is on it?" Ray fished a handkerchief out of his pocket and finally took the USB drive out of Auntie Akamai's hand.

"Files. Court documents, newspaper articles, all kinds of things. Would you like to know who they are about?" Auntie Akamai returned her arms to their crossed position and tapped her foot.

Detective Ray waited patiently.

"They appear to be about each of the D'Angelos, Ainsley Rickenbacker, and Susan Jameson." I held up a finger. "Not one about me."

"We think he was blackmailing each of them. He found out things—probably while investigating Ned D'Angelo—and was holding them ransom." Auntie Akamai's foot tapping continued.

"Investigating Ned D'Angelo," the detective repeated and looked thoughtfully at the thumb drive.

"I think we should add Heather D'Angelo just admitted to us she hired him to tail Ned, and she is the one who told my parents about Morton so they could hire him to find me." I used my hand to demonstrate the hops from person to person. "Which shows she knew him for a while, and certainly before coming here."

"They have all denied knowing Morton." Detective Ray

frowned.

"Clearly a lie, since he was blackmailing all of them."
Auntie Akamai's foot finally stilled. "At least, we think."

"Let's show you." I pointed at the resort main building.
"We can use the business office."

Auntie Akamai led the way to a small separate glass
cube with a set of computers and some chairs. Detective Ray sat
in front of one and inserted the drive while we hovered at his
sides.

Once he had it up, I pointed at each folder that was titled
with initials. "Ned D'Angelo, Heather D'Angelo, Claire
D'Angelo, Todd D'Angelo, Susan Jameson, and Ainsley
Rickenbacker."

"What's this one?" He pointed to a file that was titled
with a date.

"I don't know. I didn't open that one. Did you?" I turned
to Auntie Akamai.

She shook her head.

"Really." Detective Ray looked at me with raised
eyebrows. "Nothing relevant to that date for you, Miss
Barrington?"

Oh. "It's the date I arrived here." I grimaced. "And
please, call me Kiki."

"So perhaps there *is* a file about you?" He put the cursor
over it and clicked. "Let's take a look, shall we?"

The folder held a video. Detective Ray opened the file
and maximized it before hitting play.

We all bent toward the screen, watching intently. It
appeared to be taken at night, so it took a while to make out the
scene, but there were surfboards leaning against a building and a
stack of kayaks not quite shielding two people who were...

"Oh my!" Auntie Akamai jumped back from the
computer and looked around us wildly.

"That is *so* not me!" I gasped. "Ew!"

"But who is it?" Detective Ray actually leaned forward
to study the film of two people having, well, as my nanny would
say, "relations" against the side of a small wooden building. If
memory serves, it was the surf instructor office.

"Make it smaller, detective. What if a child walks in

here?" Auntie Akamai was swiveling her head, diligently on the lookout for minors.

Detective Ray ignored her. "Ah. Do you recognize anyone here, Kiki?"

Ugh. I leaned over his shoulder. The filmmaker was zooming in, but as the film came into focus, the woman's face became clear. "Susan!" I laughed and turned to Auntie Akamai. "It's Susan Jameson!"

Auntie Akamai was not amused.

"So who is our Romeo?" Detective Ray drug the little dot at the bottom of the picture to the right, fast forwarding it. (Which I will admit was *hilarious*.)

The person filming, most likely Joey himself, was moving to a better vantage point. As if on cue, the couple rearranged themselves and now the man faced the camera.

I gasped again. "Oh no!"

"Is that…" Detective Ray raised a hand to his forehead. "It is, isn't it?"

"Yes. Yes, it is." I took a shuddering breath. "It's Ned D'Angelo. With his new bride's *mother*."

* * *

Detective Ray had seen enough and closed that folder. We ran through Todd's file next, since it was easiest to explain. I told him what I had overheard on the pier, combined with my eyewitness evidence of Todd's drinking. He listened but didn't show any reaction.

He pulled the USB out and swiveled around in the chair to face us. "Anything else?"

"Other than saying 'I didn't do it'? Not really. I have zero motive—especially compared to those people. I knew I was going to go home at some point. It's ridiculous to think I would kill someone over that."

"Especially since all these other people from where your parents live are here." Auntie Akamai pointed out as she rolled a chair over to sit in.

"And I would need help. I could never have carried him by myself." I flexed my puny bicep and pointed at it.

"Yes, you probably would need an accomplice. Perhaps some tall, strong guy." Detective Ray stared me down.

"Ray Kahoalani, you better not be implying what I think you are." Auntie Akamai gave him the dirtiest of dirty looks.

It took me a minute, looking from face to face, to realize who he meant. "Dex? Are you kidding? I only met him that day! How would I talk a virtual stranger into helping me dispose of a body?"

"Well, witnesses do have you leaving the bar together the night of the murder." Ray crossed his legs, ankle on knee and leaned back, the epitome of relaxation.

"What?" Auntie Akamai said.

"No, no. He walked me to my room. I told him not to, but he insisted. That's all!" I glared at Detective Ray. "I'm sure the hotel has cameras that can back me up!"

Detective Ray shrugged.

Oh! "What about the boat? Do you know what boat took him out there?"

The detective's face told me nothing.

"The day I went sailing with Ned and Ainsley, there were two men arguing over a boat. One said the other took it without asking and put it back in the wrong parking spot." I clapped my hand to my head. "And when we were on the sailboat, I found a bag of diving weights that Ned subsequently threw overboard!"

This got his attention and he sat forward. "Where?"

I shrugged. "I couldn't tell you where with any accuracy."

"Why did he throw them over?"

"I said they could be evidence, and he said I was right and threw them over. I didn't do anything...but what could I do? I was out on a boat with them. They'd already knocked me overboard by that point." I frowned. *Why was I stupid enough to go with them?*

Detective Ray sat back again and studied me. "They knocked you overboard?"

"It might have been an accident. But I don't know. I don't imagine they were trying to kill me. Especially if they were planning to frame me." The waiter's words echoed in my head, and tears stung my eyes. "Ainsley and I were friends, but it was a long time ago." *I guess I didn't really trust her then. Why would I trust her now?*

"Do you know which boat the men were arguing over?"

I looked at the floor and shook my head. "Blue maybe?"

"What about the men? Could you describe them?" Detective Ray persisted with the questions.

I shook my head. "They were locals. Hawaiians."

"That's enough, Ray." Auntie Akamai's voice was soft but held command to it. "This is enough."

"One last question." Ray stood and dangled the USB on its string in front of me. "How do I know this thing isn't yours to begin with?"

I looked up at him. "You just have to trust me I guess."

CHAPTER TWENTY

————

Auntie Akamai read Detective Ray the riot act until he said he needed to make a phone call and scurried away. She had a point. If Ray trusted *her*, then he by extension had to trust me, since she brought him the drive. Which I had given her...which I wouldn't have done if I were a killer. Or something like that.

I was too busy trying to pretend like this wasn't a problem, that I was brave and strong and able to hold my own in an adult world.

I wasn't doing too well with that.

Frustrated and scared, I wandered the resort until I saw Detective Ray. I trailed him, making sure to "wander" and look at things I was passing instead of looking like I was pursuing him. I was a little surprised when he arrived at the resort pool. Another man was standing in the shade, casually keeping an eye on Susan.

Detective Ray raised a hand at the man, who in turn nodded back, then pushed off the wall he was leaning against and left.

I slipped behind a bunch of bamboo in a large pot. I was only a few feet away from Susan, but well hidden.

The detective walked up to Susan, who was reclined on a chaise lounge, and blocked the sun that fell on her face. "Mrs. Jameson."

Susan shaded her eyes with her hand and squinted up at him. A slow smile spread across her face. "Call me Susan, you big hunk of a man."

Gross!

Detective Ray nodded. "Susan...what is your connection to Ned D'Angelo?"

"He's going to be my son-in-law, isn't that a hoot? He's

older than me."

Detective Ray managed to not cringe, though I did. "And you're alright with this marriage?"

She laughed, a throaty, flirty sound. "He's filthy rich, so yeah, sure. Well, at least he was before that witch made their prenup invalid."

I leaned forward, straining to hear. Which witch?

I wasn't the only one confused, based on the tone of the detective's voice. "Who is a witch?"

"Heather. His ex-wife. She wouldn't let it be. I mean, it's not like Ned hadn't cheated on her before." Susan started laughing until tears squeezed from her eyes. She turned her head to the side to daintily wipe her eyes and spied me. She gave me a small smile.

Detective Ray persisted. "Why is she a witch? Seems to me being cheated on with a much younger woman would be quite painful for a woman her age."

Susan's eyes narrowed. "Her age?"

Detective Ray shrugged. He had to have known Heather and Susan were near the same age. *You'll get more with sugar than with vinegar*, I could hear my mother's voice in my head. It had always annoyed me, but not the phrase itself. Just that *she* said it. Like she even knew what vinegar was! But over the years, I learned the wisdom behind the words.

Susan shook it off. "She hired a PI to follow him around until he got caught with my Ainsley. She should have simply stepped aside."

Would she admit the PI was Joey?

Ray looked contemplative. "She hired a PI?"

Susan laughed harshly, the flirtiness gone. "You seemed like a pretty smart man. *Seemed.* You really haven't figured it out yet, I take it?"

Detective Ray grunted noncommittally.

Susan smiled her seductive smile again. "Puts things in a new light, doesn't it?"

"Do you think Ned had something to do with Joey's death?"

Susan shook her bleach blonde mane. "No, sweetheart. I think she did."

And she pointed directly at me.

Ray swung around to look. Annoyance, or maybe disappointment, flashed across his face, and he waved me forward. "Come on out, Kiki."

I edged out, embarrassed, but stood at the end of the chaise lounge and stared down at Susan. "I had nothing to do with Joey being killed."

"Mhm," Susan purred. "Or as I used to say to my late husband, of course, dear." She readjusted her cleavage and looked me up and down. "I mean, you are apparently not using your real name."

"It's a nickname!"

Detective Ray took a microscopic step forward, as if trying to reassert control of the conversation. "What happened to your late husband, Mrs. Jameson?"

She rolled her eyes. "He died. He was almost ninety after all." She snickered but quickly put on a sad angel mask. "He would have been one hundred and sixteen last month. At least we were able to produce Ainsley with our love."

Ew.

"And how long were you married?" Ray asked.

Susan smiled slyly. "About six months."

Ew. Ew!

"I still miss him now." She pretended to dab her eyes again.

Detective Ray and I exchanged a look, and I knew we were on the same page.

"So, Susan. Why were you arguing with Ned the other night?" I folded my arms and stared her down.

"Oh, you're a policeman too now?" Susan sneered.

"Well, my interest is piqued, and I *am* a policeman." Detective Ray turned to me. "When and where was this?"

I pointed in the rough direction. "The night before I found…him. The second night I was here." I shot a look at Susan. "The second night we were all here."

"And you know it was Susan and Ned?"

I shook my head. "I don't know for sure it was Ned, but I am pretty sure it was Susan. Someone with me, who heard too, pointed it out to me."

Detective Ray tipped his head but didn't ask who the other witness was, instead asking if the male voice could have been Joey.

That hadn't occurred to me. I pursed my lips and looked skyward. "Yes. Yes, I suppose it could have been. I was assuming it was Ned because I heard her say 'think of what this would do to Ainsley.' And I figured Ned would care, but I doubt Joey would."

The detective turned back to Susan, who seemed to be paler than before. But before he could ask, she answered.

"Okay, yes, it was Ned. I was arguing with Ned."

"About?" The detective peered over his sunglasses at her.

Susan frowned, or at least attempted to. Too much Botox. "Why do you think we were arguing? We were just conversing."

"Because I heard you. Your voice was raised and sounded angry." I swiped a bead of sweat off my neck. "*What* would do something to Ainsley?"

She shook her head in disgust. "You need to stay out of other people's business. I mean, you have enough problems of your own, being a murderess and all."

I rolled my eyes. I couldn't help it.

Detective Ray was watching the exchange and was starting to look grumpy. "Please answer the question, Susan. What were the two of you arguing about?"

Susan shrugged. "Maybe his impending arrest for tax evasion?"

"Tax evasion?" Detective Ray didn't sound particularly surprised. (And neither was I.)

"You didn't know?" Susan smiled, her lips curling cruelly.

"I didn't say that." Ray smiled back. "Tax evasion suspicions were reported by an anonymous source. Do you know anything about that?"

Panic flicked through her eyes, but she waved off the suggestion, probably pretending not to catch his question fully. "Nothing will come of it. He's a wonderful man."

I snorted. "Yes, it's clear you think he is…"

She studied me.

"Where were you later that night?" Detective Ray. I don't know how he kept his cool.

Susan played dumb, tipping her head like a confused puppy. "Oh, I don't know. Enjoying the beauty of Kauai. Like I have every night of the past week."

Ha! I'll say.

Ray raised his eyebrows. He didn't have to say a thing to raise her hackles.

"What are you trying to say, Detective?"

I snorted, a noise my mother would have had a heart attack if she heard it come out of me. "At least one night you were enjoying the beauty of Kauai, in the dark, on the beach…with Ned D'Angelo." I made a gagging motion.

Susan's face showed no expression but reddened.

"Are you going to deny an illicit rendezvous with Mr. D'Angelo on our lovely beach?" Detective Ray took over. His way of asking was much more mature than mine.

Susan glared at him and muttered under her breath.

"I'm sorry, what was that?" Detective Ray leaned in.

"It was a mistake," Susan said louder.

"Because he's going to be your son-in-law?"

She managed to arrange her face into something that might pass as a scowl. "Ainsley didn't need to know. She doesn't need to know." She flailed her arms. "Ned and I have been having an affair for close to a decade."

What?! I gasped. "Does Ainsley know?"

"No, of course not, you stupid girl. But it's the classic getting traded in for a younger version, isn't it? The version that looks exactly like you." Susan's eyes flashed with anger.

Detective Ray nodded. "So you were willing to pay Mr. Morton twenty-five thousand dollars to keep it from her?"

Susan bolted upright so quickly her bikini top almost didn't make it with the rest of her. "Who told you that? Ned?"

Ray shrugged and looked away.

As for me, my mind was spinning. But once it got away from the concept that mother and daughter had been with the same man, a lightning bolt struck. I pulled out my phone and stared at the picture of the codes. So is that the *125K*? It wasn't a number one—it was an *I* for infidelity. And they both had it.

But there was another number on her line.

"Five hundred thousand."

Both Ray and Susan turned to stare at me. I hadn't meant to say that out loud. *Whoops.* But they were both still looking at me. "So what else was Joey blackmailing you for? The twenty-five thousand must be for the beach activity. But he was blackmailing you for another five hundred thousand." I paused, looking from face to face. *What was F?* I focused on Detective Ray, willing a message to him: *Five hundred and twenty-five thousand is worth killing over.*

Ray nodded slowly, then looked back at Susan, who was staring at me with her mouth hanging open. She looked quite unattractive like that, I might add.

She woke from her shock and glanced back at the detective. "I don't know what you're talking about." She giggled.

"I do know what *you're* talking about," said Ray, looking at me over his sunglasses. "And I'm curious where you pulled that number from."

"See!" Susan burst out, pointing at me. "She knows something because she wanted him quiet too. She killed him!"

Ray's eyebrows arched. "That doesn't make a lot of sense, Mrs. Jameson. She did not appear in the evidence left by Mr. Morton. But you did."

Susan's eyes narrowed, and she abruptly reached for a sunhat from the table next to her. She jammed it on her head, far enough down to cover her eyes, and wiggled in the lounge chair to get comfortable. "I'm not speaking to you anymore without my lawyer present." Then she raised a slender arm at a passing resort worker and snapped her fingers. "Piña Colada, now!"

The worker glanced at her with widened eyes, then scurried away.

Detective Ray watched her for a moment longer, then crooked his finger at me as he turned to walk away.

I was being beckoned.

Crapola. How was I going to explain how I knew what I knew?

I started to follow him, then paused by Susan's head. "Can I ask one more question?"

"No," Susan growled from under her hat.

"I'm just wondering about Claire and Todd. Have they been in trouble?"

Susan cackled, but still didn't raise her hat. "They say the apple doesn't fall far from the tree! Now scram, you little nosey brat, before I call security."

CHAPTER TWENTY-ONE

———

"Let me give you a ride back to Auntie Akamai's." Detective Ray wasn't technically asking, more like firmly suggesting. I guess he wanted to verify I was no longer hanging around the resort and the only way to make sure was to personally remove me.

We walked to his car, and he opened the door for me. I was expecting to get interrogated about how I knew about the numbers, but he didn't say a peep until we pulled up in front of the house.

When I opened the door to get out, I could hear Paulie raising a royal racket. I paused, halfway out, and listened. He seemed really upset, squawking and shrieking loudly. Did he get out?

"Is that Auntie Akamai's parrot up there?" Detective Ray pointed through the windshield at the roof of her bungalow. Sure enough, Paulie was up there, rocking side to side and cawing. "Is that normal?"

I shook my head. "Not as far as I have seen. I've seen him outside but always with Auntie Akamai."

At that, Detective Ray was out of the car and in front of me before I knew what was happening. "Stay here."

"What? Why?" I stood, still halfway with one foot out and one foot in the car, and watched him move with a speedy grace.

He stopped abruptly on the second step, staring down, then swiveled his head around before continuing. Oddly, he walked in a circle to get to the front door instead of taking three straight steps. He knocked on the door. "Auntie! Are you here?"

Paulie was still screeching, choosing some of the more choice words Dex had taught him while keeping up his dancing back and forth.

The detective came back down the stairs, indirectly again, and looked up at Paulie. "He's got a way with words, hasn't he?"

I stepped the rest of the way out of the car and shut the door.

Detective Ray pointed at me. "I still want you to stay back, okay?"

I nodded and watched him disappear around the side of the house.

I looked up at Paulie and whistled to him. "Come here, Paulie!" I held my arm up. What is it Auntie Akamai called him? "Come here, sweetums!"

Paulie ceased his noise for a moment and cocked his head, sizing me up. "*Chicken!*"

I frowned. "I didn't call you a chicken, silly bird. Come on down here. Want a cracker?"

Paulie paused his dancing long enough to repeat "cracker" before screaming "chicken" repeatedly.

"What is wrong with that dang bird?" a woman called from behind me. It was Auntie Akamai's neighbor, who had been sitting with her a few days before.

I turned and watched her as she came across the lawn from her house. "How long has he been doing this?"

She looked me up and down. "Maybe twenty, thirty minutes now." Her head shifted to Detective Ray as he came around the other side of the house.

They greeted each other, and he asked her if she had seen anything odd that morning.

"I was hanging laundry out back when I saw a woman run through here, chasing a chicken." She waved her hand at the space between the two houses. She turned to look at me again. "I figured it was you—not sure why you were chasing a chicken if you're some fancy girl from New York. But now I see it wasn't you."

"What did this other girl look like?" Detective Ray leaned in.

She laughed. "Her." She pointed at me. "But not her."

"So, a blonde." Detective Ray passed a hand over his

eyes, a small smile on his lips.

She nodded.

"How long ago was this?"

"More than a half hour. I went out before my show started. It's done now." She squinted up at Paulie. "He was making it hard to hear my show."

Detective Ray thanked her, and she went back to her house.

"What was that all about?" I looked at Detective Ray.

"Well, someone killed a chicken and left it on Auntie's porch. I don't recommend you look at it." He stepped back to his car. "I'm calling for a crime scene investigator. See if you can get the parrot down."

I craned my neck to see the porch and could see a mound of brown. He was right. I didn't really want to see it. At least now I knew why Paulie was upset. The noise he was making might have been the noise the chicken had made during its murder. The thought made me shudder.

I shaded my eyes to look up at the parrot. He had been quiet since the neighbor had come out but was still swaying from side to side. "Come down, Paulie. It's okay. I'll take care of you."

He seemed to be weighing his options, and finally decided to come down. I held my arm out for him, cringing. He landed on my arm, sidestepped up to my shoulder, and lay his face against mine. He made some clicking sounds. *Ah, he likes me!*

"Do you want to go to my room?" I chattered nonsense to him as I walked around to my lanai, trying to get over the weird, creepy feeling of his feet on my shoulder. "I'm not sure I have anything for you to eat, but we can sit together and wait for Auntie, okay?"

After a half hour or so of waiting at my tiny table, Paulie sitting on the back of the opposite chair, Auntie Akamai and Detective Ray appeared at my door. Auntie Akamai gave a quick knock on the wood of the screen door before walking in.

"Oh, my poor Paulie!" She held out her arm, and he flew to her and they put their heads together.

"Chicken. Chicken. Chicken. Chicken." Paulie rocked and bobbed his head.

"Yes, sweetie, I know. But you're safe." Auntie Akamai stroked his back. "I'm going to take him in. And you are going to tell her." She gave Detective Ray a look.

He nodded. After she was gone, he pulled out Paulie's chair and sat. "So," he said, "there was a message left, and I believe it was meant for you. Perhaps both of you." He rubbed a hand down his face. "It looks like whoever did it may have intended to kill Paulie instead, but he got away."

"I'm very glad he did. That's horrible." My skin crawled at the thought someone could harm the bird. Or an innocent chicken. "There was a message?"

He nodded. "It was to the effect of stop nosing around or you're next."

I gasped. I honestly hadn't been expecting that. "Who would have done that?"

He shook his head. "I don't know. There was a shoe print, so maybe there will be a lead."

"And the neighbor saw a blonde woman."

He nodded. "And you were with me, so what other blonde women do we know of?"

I blew out a breath. "All of us New Yorkers, except Claire." I put a hand to my forehead. *Could this get any worse?*

"Let's go inside and get a drink of water." Detective Ray was watching me closely. "You look a little paler than usual."

"I haven't eaten recently." I looked around. "I did look around my room here, and nothing else seems to be disturbed."

His eyes went to my bed, where the suitcase still lay on its side underneath it. "I should get the CSI guys to check for prints."

I consented, and he sent me away, saying he would meet me inside.

I knocked on the back door frame before pulling open the screen. Auntie Akamai was sitting at her table, head in hands. When she heard me, she straightened and wiped at her eyes.

"I can't believe someone could have hurt Paulie to make us stop investigating." Her lip quivered ever so slightly.

"I know. And I'm so sorry. And so glad he's okay." I sat at the table with her. "Where is he?"

"I put him in his cage and covered it. He needs to rest

without stimulation." She shook her head sadly. "When they rock like that, it means they are agitated or excited." She reached out a hand. "Are you okay?"

"Yeah, I'm fine. I could use some water though. Detective Ray is having the crime lab guys look at my room, and then he's coming in too." I swiped a hand across my forehead, concerned about the clamminess.

Detective Ray joined us a few minutes later and sat at the dinette with us. "I think it's safe to say someone is bothered by what you have been doing." His eyes stopped on something behind Auntie Akamai, and he paused. "And now I see you have been doing more than I was aware of…"

He stood and walked over to the fridge and took down the list of codes Auntie Akamai had put there.

She closed her eyes and sighed.

When he looked at me, I shrugged.

"Do I want to know where you guys got these lines from?" Detective Ray stood over us, the list in his hand and a scowl on his face.

"Probably not." Auntie Akamai gave him a sweet smile. "But we wouldn't mind telling you what we've figured out from them."

"Well, Kiki made it obvious earlier." He gave me a look and gave Auntie Akamai a CliffsNotes version of the poolside conversation with Susan. "So when she asked about the monetary amounts, I had a clue you had seen this." He held up the list again.

I nodded. "And now we know why Ned and Susan had a similar section. It was because of infidelity with each other."

"It was an *I*, not a one?" Auntie Akamai gestured at the list, and Detective Ray sighed but handed it to her. "Look at that. Huh." She looked up at me as she handed the list back to Ray. "So do we know what Susan's *F* is for?"

I started to shake my head, then looked at Detective Ray with the question on my face.

"No, I haven't had a chance to look at the documents close enough yet. But tell me what you know from the rest of the lines." He laid the sheet on the table and pointed at the first line and read it. "ND-TE1/2M,0/I25K,0."

"Ned D'Angelo, Tax Evasion, one half million, infidelity, 25 thousand." Auntie Akamai recited it, then pointed. "We don't know what the 'comma zero' means."

Detective Ray read the next line aloud. "CD-CC10K,com/S&T75K,0."

I shook my head. "We know it's Claire and maybe *CC* means college cheating. No idea about the rest, or why hers has a *,com* behind that first part. The *T* probably means theft though."

Detective Ray looked at it a moment longer. "Maybe *com* means *complete*. Like her payments for that blackmail activity were done. So the *,0* in the others could mean no payments made. Which makes sense with the last part of Ned's because it just happened."

Auntie Akamai and I both said "ah" and nodded.

Auntie Akamai touched the paper on the next line, *TD-DD,R,R?25K(10K)*. "Todd was surely in trouble for drunkenness. We don't have a theory for the *R* though, or why there's a number in parentheses."

"Maybe it's the amount he had paid, as opposed to *0* or *com* like the others," Detective Ray suggested.

I nodded. "And Heather is *HD-CC50K,com*, so college cheating and completed payments."

Auntie Akamai held up a finger. "You know what I thought about at lunch? That this whole mess—this whole list— is Heather's fault. Could be, I mean. If she hadn't hired Joey to investigate her husband, he may never have found out all these other things about the family."

"Wow, you could be right." I chuckled. "I'm not about to tell her though."

Detective Ray shook his head. "I don't recommend it." He tapped the next line. "Susan Jameson. SJ-F500K/I25K,com." He paused. "Wait. This says *com*, like her payment for the beach time was made." His finger tracked back up to Ned's line. "But Ned's was not." He rubbed his chin and gazed into the distance.

"Do you know what Ainsley's is?" Auntie Akamai was looking at me. "AR-D10K,com."

I shook my head. "No clue. *D* is for…divorce? Driving… Drinking. Dieting. Being dumb?"

Detective Ray came back to the conversation. "Drugs."

I frowned. "Oh, I don't think so. It would have to be pretty heavy drugs for it to be something to be blackmailed over." I shook my head. "I don't think so."

He shrugged. "Rich and bored party girl? Who knows."

I stared at the paper. "It has to be something else. She doesn't seem like the type."

A voice called to Detective Ray from the front door. "I'll be right back."

Auntie Akamai looked at me. "He doesn't seem too upset."

"Too upset?" I shook my head. "He was none too happy when Susan pointed me out at the pool. But yeah, he doesn't seem to mind if we are sharing information."

"Well," said Auntie Akamai, "we gave him what we know and the USB drive, so we can wipe our hands clean of it now. No more birds getting threatened, okay?"

I nodded. "Okay."

Detective Ray walked back in. "They are finished out there. They cleaned up as much as they could, but you might need to do more." He turned to me. "I am going to summon the D'Angelo family and the others to meet with me. I'd like you to come along so it won't look suspicious."

I pursed my lips. "I guess it's okay. But how do you know they'll show up?"

"I'll tell them if they don't, they will be picked up and taken to the police station. They can't all possibly lawyer up in time."

Auntie Akamai tutted. "You don't need Kiki there."

He tipped his head. "I'd like them to think it is about gathering evidence on her."

She frowned. "So you're using her like bait?"

"It will be perfectly safe. We'll do it in a conference room at the resort, and I'll bring some other officers with me. It will be fine."

CHAPTER TWENTY-TWO

———

I poked my head into the conference room. It was a large room, a few chair racks full of chairs and some huge, covered rectangular shapes in a corner. There were chairs arranged in a circle in the middle of the room, but the policeman himself was nowhere to be seen. I sat in one and waited. *Will they actually come?*

I also wondered why he would want them all here together. Don't police usually like to split the suspects up, to get individual stories?

The "D'Angelo Family, Original Version" arrived first. Heather strode in, closely followed by Claire with Todd trailing behind. Todd weaved a little as he walked and immediately sat with a great sigh, like he had been on his feet for days. I could smell the booze on him from six feet away.

Heather sat next to her sotted son, which forced Claire to either sit next to me or away from her twin. Without acknowledging my existence, she sat in the chair to my left.

After a few minutes, Susan waltzed in with Ainsley on her arm. Much to Susan's chagrin, Ainsley sat primly next to me, so Susan gave me a good long glare and sat on her other side.

A few moments later, Ned sauntered in. He faltered when he saw the only place left to sit was between his ex-lover and his ex-wife. He gestured at Susan to move so he could sit next to Ainsley, and she surprisingly did so, and he ended up between his fiancée and future mother-in-law. The future mother-in-law that was just a bit more than *just* a future mother-in-law.

Ned sat, stretched out his legs, and crossed them before turning his head toward me. "What exactly are *you* doing here?"

I shrugged. "Same as you."

Ned grunted and turned to Ainsley. "Check her for a wire."

"What?" Ainsley turned to her fiancé. "How do I do that?"

"Look down her shirt and pants." Ned nudged her. "Go on."

Ainsley leaned over to me. "Sorry, but may I look down your shirt?"

I rolled my eyes and stood, lifting my shirt over my head and turned in a circle for everyone to see, then dropped it again. I gave her a "try me" look.

"Oh...okay." Ainsley looked back at Ned. "There's no wire."

"I see that." He gave me a once-over. "Nowhere else to put one, really."

I sat back down in my chair, and when I glanced back at Ainsley, she mouthed at me, *I like your bra. Gucci?*

"So, where's the cop?" Claire swiveled around, looking. "Why are we here?"

"There are only seven chairs. Maybe he's not coming." Heather looked around the room like she owned it.

"Why are we here?" Claire asked again.

I laughed. "I'm sure you all realize why you are here."

The group as a whole mumbled. Except Claire, who laughed.

"Are we here to give character witness for you, the murderess? Because that's not going to go very well." Claire managed to sound gleeful and glower at the same time.

"I didn't murder Joey." I looked around at the group. "But one of you in this circle did."

Again, incoherent mumbling from the group and a snort from Claire.

"You're kidding, right?" Claire stood and made a lazy wave at me but addressed the group. "All the evidence points to her." She looked at me. "You were practically caught red-handed."

Susan looked at her. "And what evidence is that? What exactly are *you* aware of that you haven't shared?"

Claire crossed her arms in a perfect example of

defensive body language. "She had some of his property in her little screened-in shack."

I raised my brows at her. "And how would you know that?"

Claire raised her chin defiantly. "I, uh, heard it."

"And how do you know where I live? I never told you."

She smiled like a shark, much like her mother had that first day on the boat. "Ainsley told me. *And* it was in that waste of trees called a newspaper."

She looked so hoity-toity I wanted to stand and look at her in the eye but knew it wouldn't help. Besides, I like my face the way it is. She might be a little rich princess, but this girl was not afraid to throw down.

"Sit, Claire." Heather gave her a look I was glad was not directed at me.

Claire sank back down onto her conference room chair.

"As I was saying before I was rudely interrupted, someone in this room is a murderer." I looked around at each face again. "I myself have no motive, despite the stories you tried to tell the detective. I have evidence—which I've turned over to the police—that each and every one of you was being blackmailed by Joey Morton. And that, people, is motive."

You could've heard a pin drop. (As if anyone walks around with pins. Makes more sense to be *pens*.)

Then, after a brief moment of silence, several of the group started laughing.

"You don't have anything," Todd slurred as he stood and pointed a finger. "You can't prove a thing. My dad made sure of that."

"Todd! Sit down." Claire grabbed his sleeve and pulled him down, causing him to fall.

"Oh for goodness' sake, is he always drunk these days?" Ainsley sighed. "Looks like I dodged a bullet." She reached for Ned, but he gave her a glare, which made her shrink back.

"He drinks because of you, you stupid vapid idiot!" Claire snarled and jumped to her feet.

Ainsley rolled her eyes. "Those words all mean the same thing, so who's stupid now?"

Susan decided to jump into the fray, though she

remained sitting, legs crossed lazily. "Maybe he drinks because of the way you use him, Claire!" She pointed an overly long, manicured fingernail at Claire. "Ainsley told me all about the little setup you two had going. You two would slip people roofies, then when they were knocked out, you'd rob them blind. A true crime syndicate."

"Huh?" asked Todd, looking around. "What?"

"That's a lie!" Claire stalked over to Susan and leaned into her face, then made a show of turning and pointing at Ainsley. "Your daughter does drugs!"

I gasped. *Ah, that* is *what D means.* This was like watching the finale of a juicy drama.

When Ainsley stood to refute, Claire preempted her by moving her aggressive stance to in front of her. "And at least my parents were actually married!"

"What?" Ainsley looked back and forth between Claire and her mom. "What? Mom?"

Susan waved a hand, swatting Claire's comment away like a fly. "Don't worry about that, Ainsley. Your parents were certainly married. She's a compulsive liar. And a thief. She can't even control herself when on vacation! I told you…" She turned to glare at Ned. "Daddy makes all their boo-boos all better."

I can't believe they are saying all this in front of me!

"Hey." Ned, who had until now sat and watched the arguing like it was a tennis match at the Garden, stood and held out a hand. "Let's not get carried away." He tipped his head in an obvious gesture to me.

I just sat and watched. It was like watching a car accident, but kind of an enjoyable one. Like bumper cars.

"Don't tell us what to do!" Susan narrowed her eyes to slits.

"Oh, yes, the woman who only listens when it's convenient for her. Well, listen to this: Does your daughter know you've been messing with my husband for decades? And I said 'been' as in present tense."

Every face in the room swung to look at Heather after she dropped that bombshell.

"Neddy?" Ainsley stood, swaying and reaching out a hand to Ned.

He ignored her. His face had drained of color as he stared at Heather. Who knows why it mattered to him at this point. "You knew?"

Heather laughed or, more accurately, cackled. "Of course. I'm not the only one in the room who marries for money." She turned to Ainsley and Susan in turn and gave them each a pointed look before setting her sights on Ned again. "Are you even sure Ainsley here is not actually your daughter?"

And down went Ainsley in a dead faint.

Susan screamed as Ainsley fell, then launched herself at Heather, claws out. The two fell in a pile of bare limbs and bleached hair.

I was sitting, mouth hanging open. This was a disaster! Well, for *them*.

Suddenly, over the mayhem there was a scream. Startled, I looked up at Claire, who was standing on the chair next to me, her fists clenched at her sides.

"*Everyone stop*!" She was pretty loud for a small-statured woman.

Frozen like reclined statues, Heather and Susan stopped, mid hair-yank. Susan was on top and had obviously gotten a few scratches in with those nails, while one of her eyes appeared to be puffing up. I wonder if she could cover a black eye with her makeup.

Ned was standing, arms hanging at his sides, watching the fight with odd interest. I leaned over to see Ainsley, who was still out cold on the floor. Interesting where Ned's attention lay.

Claire, still standing on her chair, lowered her voice. "Everyone calm down. We need to work together here and…" She started laughing like this was the funniest thing ever. She plopped down onto her chair again.

I wondered what she stopped herself from saying.

Todd was also sitting but looking massively confused. The freeze was broken when he turned to his sister and retched, just missing her shoes.

This got the room going again, as Claire leapt away, cursing. Heather and Susan rapidly crawled and rolled away. Ned put a hand to his head.

I too jumped away to the far side of the circle. Ainsley

was still unconscious, but I saw a twitch, so I kneeled next to her and gently tapped her cheek. "Ainsley?"

Todd, for his part, apologized and started crying until he noticed me over Ainsley. "Wass she doin' on the floor?"

I began to wonder if Ainsley was faking it. This seemed like a long time to be unconscious.

"Alright. Claire and I don't agree on much, but I do agree on that. How would it look if the police walked in right this moment?" Heather glared at each person as she returned to her chair, straightening her blouse.

Everyone else returned to their seats, Claire kindly taking mine and leaving her soiled one for me. Heather and Susan were worse for wear. Susan had a broken stiletto, the darkening eye, and very messed up hair. Heather had several scratches on her face, chest, and arms, a few of them bloody, and was rubbing her head.

Ned had turned when Todd pointed out Ainsley and finally noticed his betrothed. He sighed, then bent and gathered her limp body into his arms. He set her back on her chair, pushing her left and right until he found the balancing point for her to stay upright. Her mother watched with bland interest.

Ned caught her watching. He gave a glance around to see if Heather was watching, then leaned in. "She's not really my daughter, right?"

Susan snorted and turned away.

He leaned closer and whispered more harshly. "*Susie!*"

Susan turned back and gave him a withering look. "You really don't think I'd tell you? Especially when I found out you were *with* her?"

The fact he had to ask her made my stomach turn. *Disgusting*.

"Sit down, Ned." Heather pointed at the chair. "We need to know what this little girl thinks she knows." She turned her head toward me. "We're waiting."

CHAPTER TWENTY-THREE

———

"Okay, so each of you have motive. And you yourselves have explained away some of the evidence I have, so I thank you for that." I stood and turned in a circle as I spoke. "So does anyone have the urge to confess any more sins?"

"What I did was not a sin, Katherine." Heather was still primping her hair. "It was simply a Mother Bear watching out for her cubs."

Ned chuckled. "Lying is certainly on the list of sins, sweetheart."

"Don't call me sweetheart," she shot back. "You're probably the worst one of all of us. No morals at all." She gestured at Ainsley as she said that. "I wouldn't be the least bit surprised if you did kill the man."

Ned rolled his eyes. "I told you I didn't."

"You've told me a lot of lies."

"Okay, okay." I held up my hands. "Settle down. Do you want to hear my thoughts—which will likely be the same things the detective will think, since we've seen the same evidence. So?"

The crowd nodded and grumbled assent.

I started by pointing at Ned. "You have a lot to lose, monetarily and reputation-wise. But seeing some of your loss"—I nodded a head toward Heather—"has already occurred and the federal government is already breathing down your neck, I don't see you as needing to kill Mr. Morton. Sort of too late for it."

Ned smiled. "See?" He jeered at Heather.

"But…" I held up a finger. "Would you kill to protect someone else?"

Claire snorted. "No. He's willing to pay people off to keep his reputation clean, but he doesn't care enough about any of us to kill." She turned to the still limp Ainsley but laughed. "Even my new mommy. Sorry, not sorry, Ains."

"Okay. If I may continue." I turned to Heather this time. "You just admitted to Mama Bear tendencies. And you knew where to find the dive weights, since you went on that same diving trip as me. But are you capable of murder?"

Heather stared at me through slitted eyes.

"No, in my opinion, I don't think so. Plus, no offense, but you would need an accomplice to lift his body." I paused.

Heather looked mighty offended but kept her mouth clamped shut.

"Now, since Ainsley can't defend herself, I'll only say unless she was working with someone else—mainly Ned—I don't see her as murderous." I shrugged when no one refuted that.

"Claire and Todd." I turned toward them now. "It seems to me you are both being blackmailed for decent amounts of money, which I assume you get from your father." I glanced at Ned, who was staring at his feet. "The police are surely going to pass on the documentation to the authorities at home, and I think they are getting a warrant to search your room here at the resort as we speak, Claire."

Her mouth opened and closed like a fish, and she glared but said nothing.

"It sounds like you have a problem with taking things that are not yours." I watched her closely.

Claire kept her face blank.

"The police will find out when they search your room." I waited a few beats longer. "But other than being a thief, are you a killer?"

Ned sat upright. "You need to stop this…this…ridiculousness. My daughter did not kill anyone!"

I turned to face him. "Then who did?" Then I pivoted to look at Todd.

Todd stared at me, or probably several versions of me, with glassy eyes.

"Todd. You are pretty much…" I paused dramatically, tamped down a giggle but tried to make it look as if I was searching for the right word. "A failure."

"Hey!" Ned started to stand again, then slumped back down. "Never mind," he mumbled. He glanced at Heather and shrugged. "You're not wrong."

Claire's eyebrows shot up, and a ghost of a smile passed over her lips. When she saw I was watching her, she turned her face into a scowl.

I turned back to Todd. "You can probably be charged with multiple counts of drunk and disorderly, not that that is anything new to you. But you were being blackmailed, and you are a strong-looking kid." I waved a hand at Claire. "Perhaps the two of you were in a bigger mess than I have found."

"Huh?" Todd looked at the floor. "Yeah, sorry about the mess."

"You, I can see helping someone. Being an accomplice." I stared at Todd, but Todd probably didn't even know where he was, let alone what I was getting at.

Heather, though, made a tiny shrieking sound.

I turned and looked at Susan. "Someone who can be very convincing. Someone who has a certain mojo she works on men."

Susan gazed back at me, completely nonplussed. "Mmhum."

Her attitude annoyed me. "You had way more to lose financially to Joey than anyone else here. A *five hundred thousand dollars-worth* secret." I shot a glance at Ainsley.

"Really?" Heather looked at Susan. "What'd he have on you?"

"One is very clear, since it involves photos." I pointed from Susan and Ned and made the universal sign for vomiting. Then I turned back to Susan. "But the other, a very large amount, is not as clear. Would you like to enlighten us?"

"Not on your life." Susan crossed her arms and scootched down a smidge in her chair.

Actually, I think I might know.

"Wait a second." Heather raised her hand like a schoolgirl in class. "Why did you point at them and say there were photos? Is this old news?" She shot a look at Ainsley, who was still (probably) acting passed out.

"No, Mom," Claire snarled. "Ainsley had a 'migraine,' so

the jerk was out on the beach with her the first night we all arrived. Going at it like rabbits. So disgusting."

There was a collective intake of breath from the group. Ainsley also gasped and shot upright in her chair. "*What?!*"

I didn't gasp because I had seen those sordid, mind-bleaching photos. *But wait...*

I turned to Claire. "How did you know that?"

Claire was good at making her face blank. "What?" She shot a look at the now-sobbing Ainsley.

"Those pictures were on Joey Morton's USB drive. You saw them!" I pointed at her excitedly. "It proves you were the one who put the drive in my suitcase! After stealing my clothes!"

"Or," said Claire, distain dripping from her words, "I saw them getting it on and went and got Joey to take pictures."

Heather turned to her daughter, the hurt evident on her face. "Why would you do that? To me? To your best friend?"

Claire laughed. "Some best friend. Besides, if it got some of my blackmail forgiven..."

Ainsley cried louder. Ned frowned and edged his chair a little away from hers.

"But it's still less money to you in the end." I glanced over at Ned. "Sorry, but...you know."

Ned shrugged.

Ainsley stood and staggered over to me, holding out her arms. "You're the only one I can trust!"

I didn't hug back, as she was doing enough for the both of us. She was squeezing me incredibly tightly, pushing my neck into her shoulder until I began to see stars. I waved my arms around, and Ned jumped up and pulled us apart.

Then she started shrieking. "This is all *your* fault," she screamed at me. "Why can't you just admit you did it and leave us all alone!"

Ned sat her firmly in her chair, but she kept wailing. "I always knew you were jealous of me! You are not a friend. You should have said you did it and left us out of it." She took a jagged breath, wiping her nose on her sleeve. "Now I have nothing. No fiancé, no mother, no best friend, no boyfriend!" She had been looking at each person in turn, and when she got to Heather, she just huffed out a breath.

"Why in the world would I do that?" I shouted back at her. "You really think I'd take the fall for any of you?"

"Well, you would get away from those parents of yours that way," Susan calmly pointed out.

"Oh, stop it." I glared at her. "In case you couldn't follow what I was saying, the police are going to think you killed Joey and Todd here helped you get rid of his body."

She laughed but pulled on her earring. "You are so delusional."

"Am I? What was Joey blackmailing you over? I believe fraud, but what kind of fraud?" I looked around the group. "What kinds of things are fraud? Writing bad checks?" I looked back at Susan and watched her carefully. "Or some kind of fraud where you say you're married to someone but you never actually were?"

There were several gasps around the room and then laughter.

"Really, Susan? You were never married to that obscenely rich old man? But still got all his money?" Heather started clapping her hands. "You deserve a round of applause. Good job."

"Mom?" whispered Ainsley, staring at Susan with wide eyes

"Oh, like you have a place to criticize me!" Susan turned on her daughter and gestured at Ned. "Look what you did! Not only was that jerk my boyfriend, but he's your best friend's dad!"

Heather laughed. "Hey, you're one to talk. The jerk was my *husband*!"

Susan looked back at her. "Ha ha ha. He cheated on you with me *and* my daughter!"

"Ew," said Todd, looking like he might throw up again. "That's super gross."

"Hey now, don't bring me into this." Ned gave a halfhearted, nervous laugh.

Todd turned to him. "Did you even think about the fact that she was my girlfriend, Dad?" He looked around the circle. "And you all wonder why I drink."

"Seems to me you're the biggest victim here." I nodded at Todd. "But also an easily pliable one."

"Thanks?" Todd looked confused.

"So did you help the murderer?" I asked him point blank. His face contorted.

"You don't exactly owe any of these people anything, Todd." I waved my hand to encompass the group. "Did you help one of them kill Joey?"

He looked at his feet and nodded his head ever so slightly.

The room fell silent for a moment as the group pondered this.

"You'll have to say it out loud, not just move your head."

Every head swiveled to the new voice and watched as Detective Ray and two uniformed policemen stepped out from behind those storage containers.

"Wait!" Ned jumped to his feet. "He's drunk! That confession won't stand up in court!"

Detective Ray waved him off. "He'll sit in the drunk tank long enough to sober up, and then we'll ask him again. Seems it wasn't hard to get him to admit it if an untrained civilian got a confession out of him." As he spoke, he gestured the uniformed police to Todd.

Heather and Claire both jumped to their feet. Both shouted, "No!"

But only one kept talking.

"It was me. I confess. I did it!" She sobbed, throwing herself on Detective Ray. "He was very minimally involved, only helped me lift him. Katherine's right, I couldn't lift him by myself. But no more. He wasn't even sober, probably doesn't even remember!"

Detective Ray made a face, sighed, and handcuffed Heather D'Angelo.

CHAPTER TWENTY-FOUR

———

"That is *insane!*"

Samantha's face was shocked and impressed at the same time. There were murmurs around the table. "I can't believe there are people like that! They're like a soap opera!"

The others around the table—Samantha's friend Alani, Luke, and Casey—all murmured various things.

All except Dex, who sat with his arm around me protectively but with a stony face. "I can't believe the detective put you at risk like that."

I waved off his concern. "They were there the whole time."

"But you didn't know!" Dex argued. "He could have put you in danger. And don't say you know those people and they'd never hurt you. Clearly they are not the same people you knew in high school."

The others around the table nodded.

"Well, they kind of are. Minus the whole 'your dad is my boyfriend' part." I shook my head. "I always felt like I should be on watch around them." It helped that my mother had taught me not to trust.

"Do you think it was really the mom and her son?" Alani brushed back some of her gorgeous black hair with her hand when she spoke. I noticed how Luke watched her. I wondered absently if that was how Dex watched me.

"It sounded like it. As soon as they led her away, the others were talking about how she was trying to frame her ex-husband and his new wife for it. That makes sense, really, especially after seeing the dive weights on his boat."

"And you said there was a long blonde hair on the body." Samantha added. "The mom had long blonde hair?"

I nodded. "And whoever put the chicken on Auntie Akamai's porch was a blonde woman too." I frowned. "Though never in a thousand years did I think I'd see Heather D'Angelo catching a chicken, let alone killing one with her bare hands." It did make sense though, if she headed over after Auntie Akamai's and my conversation with her that morning in an effort to silence us.

After a while, the group made excuses that they needed to go, leaving Dex and me alone at the table.

"Lighten up." I nudged him with my elbow.

"I don't like that he did that." His brow was still pulled down.

I reached up and rubbed his forehead to make the frown go away. "Hey, at least you didn't just find out I had a fiancé I hadn't mentioned yet. Or that we went to the same college but I hadn't even told you I had gone to school…" I tipped my head and gave him a look.

"What?" Dex stared at me. "I'm confused."

"Where did you go to college?"

"In Seattle." Dex leaned back to get a better look at me. "Why?"

"Because I mentioned to Auntie Akamai where I went, and she said that's where you went as well!" I rubbed at a nonexistent spot on the table. "And that you had a fiancée."

Dex shifted his feet. "Well, okay. Yeah. Was I supposed to tell you?"

I sighed. "I thought you would have. But maybe I was wrong." I looked up at his dark eyes, lit by the fairy lights and tiki torches. "Why did you not mention college though? Is thinking about your ex that painful?"

Those eyes wouldn't meet mine. "Yes, it is."

"Oh." *Well, I guess that is that, then.* "All right. Well, I'm pretty tired. I'm going to head to bed now." I swiftly stood and started away, wanting to be anywhere but here. Last thing I needed was to get involved with someone still in love with someone else.

"Wait," Dex said but didn't even stand up to follow me.

* * *

It was hard to go to sleep, but after the adrenaline rush, I was exhausted. Good thing I had reason to cry myself to sleep.

But it seemed like mere minutes later when I was wakened by a funny scratching sound.

My eyes flew open and listened as it happened again. It sounded vaguely like someone filing their nails. *You just need a manicure*, my sleepy mind told me. *Go back to sleep.*

Nope, there it was again.

I sat up in time to see something coming toward my head. There was a blinding flash of pain and then blackness.

When I woke again, my wrists were tied to the bedframe. "What? Who?" I looked around the room—slowly, as when I tried to turn my head quickly there was a stabbing pain. I saw a small figure sitting in one of the chairs. I could only see her outline with the moonlight outside.

She had chin-length hair.

"Claire?" I struggled to sit and found my ankles were bound as well, but I managed to wiggle my way to a sitting position.

Claire sniffled. "I need you to do something for me."

"Um, couldn't you wait till morning and ask me in a less…kidnappy way?" I tried to hold my head as still as possible.

"No, because if you say no, then I have to kill you." She raised her hands. "Well, I mean I have to help you kill yourself."

"What?" I tried hard to keep a tremor from my voice.

"Oh, Katherine." Claire stood and paced to the door, looking out into the yard. "I always thought you were a bit slow." She spun and pointed at me with something that looked like a white pipe. "But you surprised me this afternoon. You almost had it figured out."

"Your mom confessed, Claire." I gently rolled my head from right to left.

"See, there's the problem. Heather didn't do it." Claire sat in the chair again and laid the pipe on the table. "And you were supposed to be the scapegoat. Not her."

"But she confessed."

"She didn't do it, all right?" Claire's voice rose, sounding a bit manic. She quickly stood and went to look out the door, then the side wall.

"Okay. But she is willing to take the fall for you." I twisted my feet and hands around, trying to loosen the knots while her back was turned. Seems she tied me with some torn scarf or something. Wait a minute. Was this my Pashmina?! How *dare she* cut up my cashmere scarf!

Claire spun around. "For me? I never said I did anything!"

"Oh come on, Claire." I sighed. "You steal stuff, right? So you stole my stuff and left the USB drive that you had taken from Joey's room, and then called in an anonymous tip."

Claire started tapping her foot nervously. "You can't prove any of that."

A flash of a memory popped into my head. "Yeah, I think I can. You were never a hiker, Claire. You hated fitness. Yet there you were, walking on the beach away from this house with a full backpack. That must be when you took my stuff." I thought about it longer. "Is that why Ainsley took me sailing? To get me away from my room?" I felt oddly disappointed.

Her foot kept tapping away, like it was the only outlet for barely contained fury. Or nervousness. *I hope nervousness.*

After a good amount of time, she nodded. "You were supposed to be the scapegoat. We were supposed to work together to make sure the police looked at you."

I felt sick. "What, you had like a family meeting about covering up your murder?"

"Well, *the* murder. No one knows I did it." She gave a short laugh, then sobered quickly. "Well, except Todd. I thought I had him sufficiently drunk for him to black out." She raised her hands in a shrug. "We all knew one of us did it, just not *who*. Joey's murder isn't exactly a bad thing for each of us, but we needed to protect ourselves. Our assets."

"That is certifiably psycho." I shuddered. "No wonder you've turned out to be a wacko."

She laughed. "Product of my environment, naturally."

"So you guys made up stories about me to get the police to believe it was me."

"Well, not made up entirely. Just changed names." She laughed. It was a hollow, dead sound. "Ainsley, Todd, and I had a more exciting upbringing than you, I guess. Or at least that you are aware of."

Yikes. Thanks for sharing. "So you had Ainsley take me sailing to get me out of the way. But what about the dive weights on the boat? What were they doing there?"

Her laugh was much harsher now. "Let's say you were not my first choice for a scapegoat. I took pains to make it look like that witch Ainsley and the jerk I used to call a father were the killers. I put the weights there before I realized you were a better option."

"Ah. And the blonde hair on the body? Was it from the night at the bar?"

"No, her hairbrush." She sounded almost proud. "I put some in the boat too. But I did yank some for future use, if needed." She waved a hand.

"It sounds so reasonable. What changed your mind?"

She shrugged. "I realized my money source would dry up if he went to jail. I had always aimed to make it look like Ainsley alone." She shook her head. "But there's no way that dipwit has the muscle or brainpower to do murder."

"I was fairly convinced it was Susan." I continued the conversational tone we had going now. Maybe Auntie Akamai would happen to be awake and look out. "I mean, the whole blonde hair on the dead body thing."

She nodded. "Yeah, that would have been fine with me. She's a scum. Do you know what she did? I mean, you almost had it at the conference room."

I tipped my head (*Ouch!*) and thought back. "I said she wasn't married to Ainsley's father."

She pointed at me. "But you noticed she said they were? I mean, she said 'your parents were married.' But that doesn't mean she was married to the old man, or that he is Ainsley's father!"

"Really!" My jaw fell open.

Claire turned her face toward the door, and I could see the outlines of her facial expression. It was gleeful.

"Joey had a whole bunch of letters and stuff. Susan was married to some guy in a small town in the middle of nowhere. I guess she left him but was pregnant. Then latched on to old Mr.

Rickenbacker, like some *Pretty Woman* story."

"Ah." I nodded slowly. "So when they married, it was technically void because she was already married. But no one knew, and when he died, she was next of kin. All this time, she's had his money and no one knew until Joey figured it out." I wiggled my hands as much as I could without making enough movement for her to see. I had to assume she could see me better than I could see her.

Claire nodded and turned her face back to me. "Big blackmail."

"Well, maybe…" I trailed away, trying to muster enough from the drama class I had taken in school. "Maybe we can work together to frame her after all? She deserves it. And the cop trusts me."

Her body went still as she considered. After what seemed like forever she shook her head. "Nah."

"Oh." What now? *Keep stalling.* "So you killed him, but haven't told me why. And why plant the hair and all that?"

She snorted. "Why would I tell you?"

I raised my shoulders. "You're going to kill me anyway. I'm just curious at this point."

"It was insurance in case his body was found." She crossed her arms. "I hoped it wouldn't be found until long after we were gone. I didn't know there was a tourist attraction under the water with those dumb lava tubes."

"Makes sense. But why did you kill him? Was it because you were sick of being blackmailed?"

She tipped her head to the side, studying me with her arms crossed. "Okay. So it's like this. I saw him here and freaked out. I mean, what was he doing here? So I stole a master key off a maid and broke into his room and took the USB drive. I was surprised—but not shocked by any means—to see he was blackmailing all of us."

"Okay. And you wanted to end the blackmail for all of you? How sweet of you."

She snorted. "No, dummy. You realize who is paying for everyone's blackmail, right? *My dad.* My golden ticket."

"Oh." I couldn't believe how cold Claire had become. "Your inheritance. You were protecting your inheritance."

She nodded. "Don't make it sound so vile. You're set to inherit from your father, too. But I have to share with my brother."

"Actually," I said, making my biggest misstep of the night, "I'd think it would be Ainsley's inheritance as his wife. She's bound to live as long as you."

Claire moved swiftly, grabbed some kind of white tube off the table, and whacked me in the head again.

CHAPTER TWENTY-FIVE

Fight, Kiki. Fight!

I heard a grunt as my feet were tugged on. My body crashed to the floor. I couldn't help but moan. Thankfully I didn't hit my head on the cement floor.

"Geesh, what have you been eating, Katherine! You weigh a hundred pounds."

Well, I should hope so! But now was not the time to discuss appropriate weights for women my height.

"If you didn't weigh so dang much, I could've done what I planned and made you hang yourself." She grunted again as she pulled me toward the door. "I guess you're going to have to drown."

I tried to mutter something but couldn't make words come out. Oh. She'd put some of my Pashmina in my mouth too. *Dangit, I love that scarf!* I started working my tongue to expel it from my mouth and twisted my body to grab the metal bed frame with my tied hands.

Claire didn't notice until she gave an extra hard tug and the frame screeched across the cement floor with me.

"Come on. You're making this harder than it needs to be." Claire leaned over me with her weapon in hand. I was relieved to see it was PVC pipe and not metal. But it still hurt like the dickens to be whacked with it. "Let go."

I shook my head. So she wound up to take a whack at my wrist. As the pipe came down, I pulled my hands back and the metal bed frame clanged like a bell out into the night.

She straightened and stood frozen, listening. Ocean waves, insects, birds. Reassured no one had heard the sound, she resumed her pulling.

Of course, I grabbed on to the bed again, hoping to redo

the noise. This time she pointed the pipe at my head.

"You want this on your head again?"

I shook my head and let go of the bed.

She resumed pulling. By the time we got outside, I had grabbed on to the bed twice more, and then the doorframe. I think I broke a nail.

She was not amused.

"I can't keep hitting you, Katherine! The whole suicide thing. Come on. Cooperate."

This chick was nuts.

Once we were in the grass, it occurred to me if I could grab things, I could certainly pull the scarf out of my mouth. *Duh.* So as she dragged me across the lumpy grass, I formulated a plan. At least a start of a plan!

I tried to judge where exactly we were, how close to the banyan tree she would drag me. Maybe she would trip on a root, but I couldn't take the chance she wouldn't. I felt a root moving up my body as she dragged me over it, so I waited until it was at my shoulders, then flipped to my side, pulled my legs as far into a fetal position as I could, and grabbed the root with my hands. When she turned, brandishing the bat, I lunged into a sit and snatched it from her. As soon as I had it in my hand, I kicked out with my legs. She staggered backward and fell over that blessed root.

I was loose! And had disarmed her.

But I was still bound, hands and feet.

"Help!" I yelled, inch-worming as fast as I could. Mentally thanking my horrific personal trainer, I set my hands on the ground and walked my legs up until I could squat without tipping over and stood. I started hopping. "Help! Auntie! Paulie! Chicken!" I just yelled whatever came to mind, whatever might help, whoever might hear me.

I didn't get too far before Claire recovered.

"Come back here!" Claire jumped at me, catching me around the waist in a football tackle. She landed on top of me and knocked the air right out of me.

I lay there, gasping for breath. Claire had grabbed my hair and wrapped it around her hand. "Stop!"

"*Stop!*" A voice cut through the night. "*Rat fink!*"

Claire pulled my head toward her. "Stop where you are! I have a knife!"

"No she doesn't!" I struggled to get out from under her. "Help!"

"<u>Help</u>!" the voice repeated.

My heart felt like it turned to lead.

It was Paulie.

Please, please wake someone human *up.*

"Chicken!" I yelled my war cry as I swung my elbow back. I heard a satisfying crunch when it contacted with her nose. *Ha! You'll have to get a new-new nose now!*

"*Chicken*!" Paulie screamed and flapped somewhere above us as Claire screamed, falling back, waving her arms to protect herself from the so far unseen creature.

I started wiggling my way forward again, but Claire seemed to gain superhuman strength with blood loss. She grabbed me by the arms this time or, more accurately, the scarf that bound my wrists and started dragging me toward the water again.

I made it as hard for her as I could, throwing myself back and forth, hoping she would lose balance or tire out quicker. Once we hit the sand, it was easier for me to dig my heels in.

Then I heard a tearing sound and an "oof" as the scarf holding my hands together tore and Claire fell face-first into the sand. I immediately turned and began to claw my way back the way I came from, which in hindsight was not my best move. She simply grabbed my ankle bindings and kept dragging me.

But we were still in the soft sand, which made her pulling harder as well as gave me a weapon of sorts.

"Claire! Stop! You don't have to do this!" I held on to the sand the best I could. "You're going to go to jail—do you want it to be for one murder or for two?"

"I don't care!" she shouted as she turned toward me.

And I threw a fistful of sand into her face.

She cried out, dropping my ankles, and swiped madly at her face. "Why did you do that?"

Instead of trying to crawl away again, I decided I needed to hold my ground and fight. I started with another fistful of sand, and she retaliated by kicking some at my face, but being she couldn't see well with sandy eyes, she missed. So she jumped on me instead and started flailing her arms, reaching for my face.

Luckily, being taller than her meant I also had slightly longer arms, so I planted my hand on her face and extended my arms fully. She howled in pain.

Oh, yeah. I'd broken her nose. Forgot. *Whoopsie!*

Her attempts to punch me escalated. She landed one good one on my cheekbone, then grabbed my hair.

We were fighting, rolling, yelping…and managed to fight our way down to the hard sand.

The wrong way. The water was close now.

She landed a punch to my stomach, and the air was knocked out of me. She started dragging me again, and I felt the water on my body.

Is this it, then?

There were only a few inches of water, at least when the wave came in, but she held my face down in it, smushing my face into the wet sand. She used the waves to her advantage to carry me out farther. I held my breath and scrabbled at her hands on my head. Every few waves, I was able to get a fresh mouthful of air.

What if I were to play dead?

Seemed kind of lame to me, but maybe it would work. It worked for some species of fish, right? So I stopped grabbing at her hands, then a few moments later let them fall in the water next to me.

I heard her laugh as she pulled me out farther into the water, still holding my face down.

My left hand touched something slimy, and I reacted by pulling my hand back, almost involuntarily. So much for playing dead. It didn't seem Claire noticed though.

Then the slimy thing stung me. A jellyfish!

Claire's leg was pressing against my left side. I wasn't sure which way she was facing—toward my head or my other side—but I gently took hold of the jellyfish. (Which is even harder to do then it sounds!) My eyes squeezed shut from the pain of more stings, I pulled it toward her leg. I waited for a reaction.

"Ow!" Claire let go of my head with one of her hands and swiped at her legs. "Ow, ow ow!" She let go with the other hand, and I swung my left hand up toward her face and let my sea creature friend go.

Claire was screaming and clutching her face, and I rolled over, gasping for air. I started to get to my feet and felt another jellyfish sting. I scooped the water, flinging it at Claire. She ran out of the water to the hard-packed sand and collapsed to her knees, holding her face and crying.

I began to hop away, only to be blinded by a light to the face. Auntie Akamai loomed out of the darkness in a white nightgown, carrying a flashlight.

"Be careful, she's right there!" I pointed to where Claire was kneeling in the sand.

Auntie Akamai turned and frowned. Then she calmly walked over to Claire, gave her a good push to put her face first in the sand, and sat on her.

CHAPTER TWENTY-SIX

———

I don't think I had ever been so happy I had worn shorts and a sports bra to bed.

Hours later, I was finally released from the police station. Medics had treated my jellyfish stings, banged up head, swollen eye, and Pashmina lacerations. *I would never forgive Claire for destroying my favorite cashmere scarf!*

Auntie Akamai had been woken by Paulie, called the police, then set out with her high-powered flashlight. She'd then proceeded to sit on Claire until the police showed up. I'd simply sat in the sand out of arms' reach and started to feel all the pain as it rolled in like the waves of the sea.

Detective Ray had shown up as they were cutting my ankles loose. I'd noticed they put the scarf remnant in a bag and took it away.

He'd helped me up, and I'd hobbled between him and Auntie Akamai to the back of an ambulance, where I'd sat and told them the story.

"So it was Claire after all." Ray had shaken his head. "I knew it wasn't Heather."

I'd nodded. "Claire wanted me to confess to save Heather, and if I refused, she was going to kill me and make it look like suicide." I'd run through all the hindsight evidence, all those things that were in plain sight but we didn't see.

Her thievery getting her the USB, which she then planted at my place. Me seeing her immediately after her burglary, with her full backpack. Pulling out Ainsley's hair, unprovoked. Knowing about Susan and Ned's nighttime liaison.

"Did she say why she killed Joey?" Auntie Akamai had stood watching the medics like a hawk.

"To protect her inheritance. All the blackmail payments,

other than Susan's, came from one source. Ned. The more money out meant the less money she would inherit." I had winced when the medic palpitated around my eye, I'd assumed to check to make sure the eye socket bone wasn't broken. "I made the mistake of mentioning it would go to Ainsley anyway. It was like the last straw for her."

"Okay." Detective Ray had straightened. "I need you to come make a statement at the station, if you are feeling up to it?"

I'd nodded, slowly. Auntie Akamai had gotten me a T-shirt when she went in to change and had insisted on driving me. She'd bought me a scone and a cappuccino at the coffee shop across from the station. Inside, she'd sat with me as I'd recounted everything from the very beginning for the record and as I'd waited for them to type up and print out my statement.

When we finally stepped out of the station, I moaned, and my hands went up to cover my eyes. "It is so bright."

"Kiki?" Dex's voice.

"Dex?" I turned toward him and fought the sudden urge to throw myself into his arms and cry.

"Oh man, she really did a number on you." Dex came closer and lifted a hand to move my hair out of my face.

Auntie Akamai huffed. "The other gal looks worse, let me tell you. Kiki busted her nose!"

Dex gawked at me. "Really?"

I smiled, just a bit because everything hurt. "Self-defense classes." I held up my bruised elbow, which would soon match the bruises on my forearms from the sailboat boom. "The instructor told us to always use elbows. They're pointy."

"Are you okay though?" Dex took another half step closer.

"I'm not even here, am I, *keiki*?" Auntie Akamai groused before disappearing into the background.

All I could see now was Dex, standing very close to me. "Everything hurts."

"Can I hug you though? Gently?" He was speaking at a whisper.

I gave one small nod and lifted my arms to his upper arms. He wrapped his arms around me and held me against him, not squeezing me at all but holding me like I was made of blown glass.

Wow, he smelled good. As usual. I wouldn't mind getting used to this.

"I'm sorry about not telling you about college and my old girlfriend," he mumbled into my hair.

"It's okay." I tilted my head (*ow*) to look at his chin. "I had no right to get upset about it. You'd tell me when you were ready to."

Dex bent farther into his hug so his mouth was right next to my ear. "Can I kiss you now?"

I nodded and met him halfway for the gentlest kiss I have ever received. All the noise, all the pain—gone. For a few magic seconds.

"*Katherine!* Katherine Tiffany Barrington! What do you think you are doing?!"

Oh no. I stepped back from Dex a little too quickly and swayed at the burst of pain in my head. My mother stood a few feet away, arms crossed, glaring at me. My father was looking over her shoulder, but he looked amused.

When I turned toward my parents, their expressions flashed through several emotions.

My mother gasped. "What in the world..." She turned on Dex. "Young man, did you do this to her?!" She advanced on him like a Valkyrie warrior woman.

"Mrs. Barrington, Mr. Barrington, let me explain." Auntie Akamai stepped between us.

"Who are you!" My mother stuck her chin in the air and looked down her nose at her.

"I'm Mrs. Akamai. The woman who called you?"

What!? I turned to stare at Auntie Akamai.

"Oh, my goodness. Well, thank you then." My father stepped forward and took her hand. "We owe you one."

My mother lowered her chin, and I realized with a shock her lip was trembling. She nodded to Auntie Akamai. "Thank you."

"Come," said Auntie Akamai. "Let's go to my place and talk."

Dex walked with us to the car, introduced himself, and shook hands with my father. He turned to my mother and hesitated.

And she hugged him. She *hugged* him! The Ice Queen huggeth!

Then she turned to me and put a hand to my non-bruised cheek. "Oh my poor baby." Her eyes welled up with tears.

My mother…had tears?

Dex helped me into the car, then stood back. He gave me a little smile and a wave as we pulled away from the curb.

My mother sat in the back with me and *actually held my hand*. I suppose she thought no one else could hear her, but she told me she had missed me and had been so worried, especially after getting the news from Auntie Akamai about the murder.

Auntie Akamai explained she'd called them when I was at the pier with Dex. She had been worried about the evidence, but also what she had seen in my eyes when I talked about Dex.

She was worried I would never want to go home, and being a mother, she hurt for mine.

"I don't want you to leave, *Kaikamahule*. I just didn't want your parents to be in the dark any longer." She peeked at me in the rearview mirror. "You needed them."

I gave her a small nod. I wasn't going to be mad at her.

When we got to Auntie Akamai's bungalow, my father helped my mother, then me out of the car. He gave me a tentative hug before we followed Auntie Akamai inside.

Paulie squawked when he saw the visitors. My mother cringed when she saw him but warmed right up to him after he gave her a wolf whistle and said, "I am a very stylish girl." I recognized it right away as a line from my mother's favorite movie. He even imitated Audrey Hepburn's voice, and my mother was over the moon.

Once we were settled in the living room, Auntie Akamai and I launched into the whole story, taking turns telling it. My parents were alternately horrified and disgusted.

"I always knew there was something off about that girl." My mother's face was pinched. "And that woman Susan. I do hope she gets arrested for her fraud."

My father nodded. "I had heard whisperings of Ned D'Angelo's business practices, so that part is not surprising. But his family…" He blew out a sigh and shook his head.

My mother turned to him. "But taking up with a girl his daughter's age?!"

My father made a face. "Technically a woman, dear. Just like our daughter."

My mother's head tipped, and her eyebrows shot up.

"Well, of course much too young. That goes without saying. I meant...legally." My father looked at me, hoping I'd save him. "She's legally an adult."

Mother joined him in looking at me. Their faces were impossible to read.

Auntie Akamai immediately picked up the new vibe. "I, oh, need to...go in the kitchen. Coffee. I'll make coffee." And she fled the room.

My parents still gazed at me. I couldn't tell if they were sad, or mad, or disappointed.

I was going to go with disappointed. That honestly is the worst of the three as well as the one I was most accustomed to.

"I'm sorry I left and didn't tell you where I was. I realize now it was foolish." I had my hands folded in my lap and stared at the scarf lacerations on my wrists.

There was silence until I looked up.

My father spoke first. "Why did you leave?" My mother started to say something, but he shot her a look. "Did you feel like I was pressuring you to work for me?"

I nodded. "Yes. And...I'm really sorry, but I don't want to."

He laughed. "That's no surprise, Katherine. The only time you ever seemed interested in my work was when you asked if there was a dive shop involved."

My mother stayed silent.

"Speaking of a dive shop...Mrs. Akamai told us you got a job at one." My father fidgeted. "Is that the type of work you want to do?"

"Yes. It's what I studied. I love the water, the creatures in it. I feel at home under the sea." I hesitated when the look on his face suddenly became sad. "I'm sorry," I added quickly.

He gave a little smile. "Don't be sorry. I'm happy you can work in a field you love. Following your passion. It's an amazing thing to be able to do."

Oh. He doesn't love his job. I had never considered whether or not he enjoyed it.

"I agree." My mother sighed. "Not everyone can do what they dream of."

I looked at her, perplexed. I thought my mother dreamed of blue-hued boxes and the sparkly things inside. Did she have another side to her? "What do you dream of?"

She gave a short laugh and was saved by Auntie Akamai coming back in the room with a tray of her Kona coffee. "That's a story for another day."

Auntie Akamai poured the coffee, and we had a perfectly civilized conversation, moving on from murder and regrets. After an hour or so, my eyes began drooping, despite the Kona, so my parents made moves to excuse themselves and headed to the resort. They would stay a few days to make sure everything was straightened out with the legal issues. Before they left, Mother and I exchanged air kisses (more the norm than the hugs and hand holding), but my father kissed me on the cheek.

I watched them drive away with a smile.

Auntie Akamai put an arm around my shoulders. "They weren't so bad. Why did you make them sound so awful?"

"I'm not sure those people were actually them. I think there was some invasion of the body snatchers stuff going on." I yawned.

"Perhaps they thought they had lost you."

I turned to her. "Thank you, Auntie Akamai."

"Of course, *Kaikamahule*. Now, I want you to sleep in the guest room over here so I can keep an eye on you. Doctor's orders. Okay?" She pointed down the hall. "Go on, girlie."

I headed the direction I was told, but stopped to turn back. "What does it mean, what you called me?"

"*Kaikamahule*?" Auntie Akamai smiled. "Niece. It means niece."

ABOUT THE AUTHOR

Rosalie Spielman enjoys moving in order to clean out her closets. After meeting her husband when they were both in the Army, they moved eleven times in twenty-four years, to multiple states and three countries. Somewhere along the way, Rosalie discovered that she could make other people laugh with her writing. She finds joy in giving people a humorous escape from the real world. Her cozy mystery novels are set in locales that have chickens, such as rural Idaho and sunny Kauai.

Rosalie is an active member of Sisters in Crime and is represented by Dawn Dowdle of the Blue Ridge Literary Agency. She currently lives in Maryland with her husband and four creatures—two teens and two fur babies.

To learn more about Rosalie Spielman, visit her online at: www.rosalie-spielman-author.com

Visit

aloha lagoon

Trouble in paradise...
Welcome to Aloha Lagoon, one of Hawaii's hidden treasures. A little bit of tropical paradise nestled along the coast of Kauai, this resort town boasts luxurious accommodation, friendly island atmosphere...and only a slightly higher than normal murder rate. While mysterious circumstances may be the norm on our corner of the island, we're certain that our staff and Lagoon natives will make your stay in Aloha Lagoon one you will never forget!

www.alohalagoonmysteries.com

CPSIA information can be obtained
at www.ICGtesting.com
Printed in the USA
LVHW090054251121
704426LV00004B/570

9 798755 180627